Intruder at the Campfire . . .

The boy sitting next to Holly started to speak, but suddenly there was a bloodcurdling scream from the near edge of the woods.

An instant later the brush parted and a figure leaped into the firelight.

He was dressed in a dark shirt and pants, and a hockey mask gleamed on his face.

As Holly watched, horrified, he pulled a hatchet out of his belt and began to advance on the counselors.

Lights Out

R. L. STINE

AN ARCHWAY PAPERBACK
Published by POCKET BOOKS

New York   London   Toronto   Sydney   Tokyo   Singapore

AN ARCHWAY PAPERBACK *Original*

An Archway Paperback published by
POCKET BOOKS, a division of Simon & Schuster Inc.
1230 Avenue of the Americas, New York, NY 10020

ISBN: 0-671-72482-7

First Archway Paperback printing July 1991

10 9 8 7 6 5 4 3 2 1

Cover art by Bill Schmidt

Printed in the U.S.A.

IL 6+

Lights Out

chapter

1

Camp Nightwing

Dear Chief,

Here I am at Camp Nightwing, just as I promised. The other counselors are already here—and the lucky campers are arriving tomorrow.

Everything looks cool so far. Don't worry about a thing, Chief. I'll make them pay. Every one of them. Just as I promised you. Before I'm through, everyone will be calling it "Camp Nightmare."

I'm just trying to figure out where to start. Any ideas, Chief? Please write back and let me know what you think. I'm dying to hear from you.

Yours forever,
Me

chapter
2

The spider's shiny body glistened in a shaft of sunlight as it slid down a thread from the ceiling. At the bottom of the thread it splayed out its eight long legs all at once, then dropped onto the center of the white pillow.

"AAAGH!" With a startled cry Holly Flynn jumped back from the bunk, pulling her duffel bag to the floor. Her heart pounding, she took a deep breath, then leaned over for a closer look. The spider was about the size of a quarter.

"Go away, spider," Holly said earnestly. "Go back where you came from."

The spider ignored her. It seemed as if it might be prepared to remain on her pillow for the rest of the day, if not the whole summer.

"I *hate* this," Holly said out loud. Cautiously she approached the bunk again. "It's just a harmless spider," she reassured herself. "It can't hurt me."

She knew that what she was saying was true, but she also knew that she couldn't bear the thought of touching a bug of any sort—even to kill it. Especially to kill it. Holly's mother often said that Holly was too tenderhearted for her own good. Making a sudden decision, Holly gingerly picked up the pillow and tossed it onto another bunk. She didn't care what the spider did as long as it didn't do it on her bunk. With a loud sigh she picked up the duffel bag and returned to the task of unpacking her gear.

As she stashed folded T-shirts, underwear, and shorts in the drawers of her tiny cubby, Holly asked herself for the hundredth time that morning what she was doing there.

It had all started with a phone call from her uncle Bill two weeks earlier. Usually Holly was delighted to speak with her favorite uncle. But during that phone call her uncle had sounded worried, even though he was obviously trying to make a joke of everything. It turned out that he was inviting Holly to work as a counselor at his summer camp—Camp Nightwing.

"You can't be serious. I *hate* the outdoors!" Holly had protested. "You know I'm terrified of bugs and snakes."

"All the critters here are friendly," he had joked. "It'll be good for you, Holly. Get out in the fresh air, get some exercise, get you away from Fear Street."

Holly laughed. Uncle Bill was always teasing her about living on Fear Street. He thought it was funny to remind her of the grisly legends about the street. But, thank goodness, she wasn't superstitious, and she liked her old-fashioned house and the other old houses on the street.

"But I don't know the first thing about being a counselor," she went on.

"You'll learn," Bill promised in his hearty, booming voice. "Besides, you're an expert swimmer and a good sailor, and you'd be great teaching crafts." Before Holly could protest further, Bill asked to speak to her mother, his sister.

With growing misgivings Holly watched as her mother talked to Uncle Bill. She saw the crease of worry on her mother's forehead when she hung up. "Bill really needs your help," she told Holly. "His camp is barely making it, honey. Besides, you don't have any other summer plans since that job at the Dairy Freeze fell through—and it'll be good for you to be outdoors."

Bill had always been Holly's favorite uncle. He was always ready with a joke or a hug—whatever she needed most.

But Bill had always had hard luck with every business he ever started. He'd owned Camp Nightwing for the past three years, and everyone in the family hoped it would finally be the success he deserved. But things had begun to go wrong the first year. A fire started by lightning had burned down the rec hall. The second year there was a flood, and right after that an outbreak of measles had closed the camp for three weeks.

Last year, sadly, a camper had been killed in a boating accident.

As a result of those disasters, Bill was barely keeping the camp afloat. He couldn't pay as much as other camps and was having trouble hiring enough counselors. "If only he can make a success of it this year," Holly's mother pleaded. "Please, Holly, at least think about it."

Feeling trapped, Holly finally agreed. She did owe it to her uncle, after all. And besides, it might be good to get away from Shadyside for a while. Her attempts at finding a summer job had been unsuccessful. And she had just had a stormy breakup with her boyfriend, George, and she didn't want to be running into him at Pete's Pizza and the mall.

Now, two weeks later, standing in the empty cabin, she thought that if only she could learn to love snakes and spiders . . .

"Yo, anyone here?"

Holly came out of her daydreams to see her best friend, Thea Mack, standing in the open cabin doorway, her short dark curls bobbing over her expression of mock exasperation. "Are you deaf?" Thea demanded.

"Thea!" cried Holly, feeling happy for the first time that day. "When did you get here?"

"A few minutes ago," said Thea. "I was going to ask you to sit on the bus with me, but when I called your house this morning you'd already left."

"I drove down with my mom," said Holly. "She wanted to see Uncle Bill."

"It's just so hard to believe that Uncle Bill is really your uncle," said Thea, watching Holly finish her unpacking. "When I was here last year, I had no idea. I just thought he was this funny, nice man everyone called Uncle."

"I'm lucky to have him for an uncle," agreed Holly. "But, Thea, do me a favor—don't let anyone else know. Uncle Bill and I think it would be best to keep it a secret that we're related, so people won't treat me differently."

"Okay, fine," said Thea. She turned Holly's duffel upside down and shook it out over the bed. "All finished," she said. "What should I do with this?"

"Stash it under the bunk, I guess," Holly said. "Aren't you going to unpack?"

"I'll do it later," said Thea. "I'm not as organized as you. So, ready for exciting camp counseling experiences?"

"I'm just hoping to make it through to the end of the summer!" said Holly. "Thea, you know I'm not the outdoors type."

I don't even look right, Holly thought, comparing her own pale white arms to her friend's dark, freckled skin. Thea was the perfect image of an outdoors athlete, with her compact, muscular build and short hair. Holly, on the other hand, was long and lanky with fine pale hair. An indoors type if there ever was one.

"Don't be silly," said Thea. "That's just what you tell yourself. But I know you're a good swimmer, and you just need experience with the other stuff. Just be sure to wear plenty of sunscreen when you go out."

"Right," said Holly.

"Really," Thea insisted, "this can be a wonderful opportunity for you. And if you're not interested in the outdoors, well, there are plenty of other attractions here."

"Like what?" said Holly.

"Like some really good-looking guys," said Thea.

"I know about the one you have the thing for— what's his name—John?"

"John Hardesty," said Thea. "Yeah. I had fun with him last summer. He's supposed to be back this year, but I haven't seen him yet."

"I can't wait to meet him," said Holly. "You've talked about him enough."

"He's not the only one either," Thea went on. "The archery counselor is a real babe, and there's a new boating instructor who—"

"Forget it," Holly cut in. "After George, I'm on vacation from boys for the whole summer. In fact, that's one of the reasons I decided to come."

"Don't be too sure," said Thea. "There might be so many guys to choose from that you'll—"

But before she could say more, a piercing cry rang through the camp.

"Help!" a frantic, terrified voice called. "Help! Someone please help me!"

chapter
3

"*H*elp!" the voice cried again. "Please, someone help!"

Holly felt as if her heart had stopped.

The voice belonged to her uncle Bill!

"Come on!" she told Thea. Without waiting for an answer, she bolted out of Cabin Five, running hard toward the main building across the road.

Uncle Bill's cries were coming from the rec room, which was a big, screened-in area at one end of the mess hall. "Over here!" she called to Thea.

Holly yanked open the big screen door, and she and Thea ran into the room. At first all she could see was a big pile of sports equipment. Catcher's mitts, tennis rackets, volleyball and badminton nets, and balls of every sort were piled in a huge jumble in the center of the floor.

And then she saw that teetering over the pile was a huge metal cabinet, attached to the wall on one side and completely loose on the other. Uncle Bill was buried under the sports equipment, his leg trapped under the loose side of the cabinet.

"Uncle Bill!" Holly cried, kneeling by him. "Are you all right? What happened?"

"I think I'm okay," Bill said, grimacing. "But I need help. I was checking the equipment out when the cabinet just came loose. I was afraid if I tried to move it, the whole thing would pull out of the wall and come down on top of me."

"Just hold still," said Holly. "Thea and I will move it off you." She and her friend pushed the sports equipment aside, then took hold of the loose side of the cabinet and, pushing as hard as they could, gradually righted it. Peering inside the empty cabinet, Holly could see where the bolts had come loose.

While Thea held the cabinet to make sure it didn't fall again, Holly helped Bill to his feet. There was a big red mark on his calf where the cabinet had had him pinned, and he winced when he stood on that foot.

"Are you okay?" asked Holly. "Do you need a doctor?"

"I'm fine," said Bill. "Just a bruise. Thanks a lot, girls. I didn't feel like spending the rest of the day on the floor." He walked over to where Thea was holding the cabinet. "Now, let's see what's going on here," he said.

Holly and Thea watched while Uncle Bill inspected the cabinet, moving the free end forward and backward. "This is the strangest thing," he finally said, partly to the girls and partly to himself. "Do you see how this is designed? With bolts at all four corners?"

Holly and Thea nodded. "I had my handyman make it that way so it would never pull out of the wall," Bill went on. "Even in a heavy thunderstorm with high winds, it should stay smack up against the wall. But somehow—somehow the bolts on one side worked loose. I just can't understand it."

"Maybe they weren't tight enough," Thea said.

"I checked them myself," Bill said. "First thing when I opened the camp last week. I always double-check everything. I don't understand it. . . ."

"You're just lucky the bolts came off on only one side," said Holly. "If the whole cabinet had fallen, it could have killed you!"

For a moment Uncle Bill seemed to be startled, then he smiled again. "You worry too much, Princess," he told Holly, calling her by his pet name. "But you raise a good point. I'd better check the other side while I'm at it." He tousled Holly's hair affectionately.

"Uncle Bill," she said. "Please. You promised if I came here, you wouldn't let anyone know you're my uncle."

"Sorry," he said. "I forgot. But you're right. We don't want anyone teasing you. I'm just sorry I'm not going to get to brag about you."

Holly laughed, feeling embarrassed.

Bill pushed a heavy table against the cabinet to hold

it up. "Well, I'd better get my tools and fix this up," he said, starting out.

"We'll neaten up all the sports gear," said Holly.

"Thanks a lot," said Bill. "I appreciate it."

"You're so lucky," said Thea after he left. "I wish I had an uncle like him."

Holly bent down and began to untangle the twisted volleyball net. "There's so much gear here," she said after a moment. "The camp has enough sports equipment for the Olympics."

"I know," said Thea. "It's a really great camp. That's why so many counselors did come back this year."

Holly was silent, thinking of what her mother had told her about Uncle Bill's troubles. I've got to do everything I can to help him this summer, she thought. No matter what.

"Where should we put all this stuff?" asked Thea.

"I don't know," said Holly. "Pile it up on the table, I guess."

She had finally managed to fold the volleyball net and was carrying it over to the table. She took another good look at the cabinet. It reached nearly to the ceiling, and she didn't want to think about what it weighed. She felt a little shudder as she thought of what could have happened to her uncle.

Thea came over with a large box filled with Ping-Pong paddles and tennis rackets. "This could take all day," she said. Then, as she set the gear down: "What's that?"

"What's what?" asked Holly.

"There, behind the cabinet," said her friend. Holly

looked where Thea was pointing and saw a flash of red. Curious, she peered behind the cabinet. In the bolt hole where the top bolt had come loose from the wall, a small red feather was sticking out.

"Now, that's weird," said Holly. She pulled the feather out and examined it. "Where in the world did this come from?"

"Who knows?" said Thea. "Maybe a cardinal flew in and decided to molt."

"Get real." Holly laughed.

"It probably came from the crafts cabin," said Thea. "There's lots of stuff like that in there—feathers, beads, leather strips."

"That must be it," Holly agreed. But she couldn't help wondering how the feather had managed to get inside the bolt hole.

In a few minutes all the sports gear was neatly stacked except for the balls. Holly took a big cardboard box and began to fill it with baseballs, basketballs, rubber bouncing balls, beach balls, soccer balls, and tennis balls. They were scattered all over the room, and she wondered if she'd ever find them all. While she worked, she half listened as Thea talked on and on about the boys at camp.

After a few minutes Holly realized her uncle hadn't come back. "What happened to Uncle Bill?" she asked, interrupting Thea's hundredth description of John Hardesty. "He's been gone awhile."

"Oh, he probably got sidetracked," said Thea. "I saw a food-delivery truck drive by a few minutes ago."

Poor Uncle Bill, Holly thought while Thea chattered on. He has to do practically everything in camp by himself.

"So what do you think?" asked Thea.

"About what?" said Holly.

"Haven't you been listening?" Thea said. "About John. What should I do when I see him? Should I let him know how glad I am to see him or play it cool?"

"Play it cool," said Holly after a moment. "At least till you see how he feels."

"I'm sure he'll be glad to see me too," Thea said. "I mean, he did write me a couple of times during the year."

"When was the last time?"

"January," said Thea. "But he's probably been busy."

"Probably," agreed Holly.

"You don't sound so sure," said Thea, frowning. "What do you really think?"

"How should I know?" Holly laughed. "Thea, I'm not a mind reader! Besides, if things don't work out with John, what about all the other great guys you were telling me about?"

"I was telling you about them for *you*, silly," said Thea. "Of course," she added teasingly, "there might be a little competition. . . ."

"You mean if things don't work out with John."

"We're not the only girl counselors," Thea said. "But I was thinking mostly about Geri Marcus."

Holly froze. *"Who?"*

"Geri Marcus."

"Short red hair, from Waynesbridge?" Holly realized she was babbling, but she couldn't help it.

"Right description," Thea said, "but I don't know where she's from. You can ask her yourself—here she comes now."

"No!" Holly cried. "Oh, no! Not here! It can't be!"

chapter
4

Holly felt as if her heart had dropped to the bottom of her toes.

When Thea had first mentioned Geri, for just one wild moment, Holly hoped that she meant some *other* Geri Marcus. But now, seeing her walk up the graveled path toward the rec room, there was no doubt.

Watching Geri's easy stride, her perfect, blunt-cut strawberry-blond hair, dazzling smile, and creamy skin, Holly felt a mixture of emotions—warmth for the friendship she and Geri had once had, and sadness and anger for the way that that friendship had ended.

"What's up?" asked Thea worriedly. "You look as if you've seen a ghost."

"In a way I have," whispered Holly as the screen door swung open. "I'll tell you about it later."

Geri held the screen open a moment, then walked in as if she owned the camp. At first her eyes narrowed when she saw Holly, then she put on an easy smile.

"Hi, Geri," said Thea. "Holly, this is Geri Marcus. Geri, I want you to meet my friend Holly—"

"I know her already," said Geri coolly. "And I had a feeling she'd be here." She walked past the two girls and stood scanning the shelves of the lending library a moment before picking up an armload of books. Then, ignoring Holly and Thea, she went back out again.

"What was that all about?" asked Thea when Geri had gone.

"It's a long story," said Holly. She sighed and sat on a camp stool, thinking about it. Even now, almost two years later, Holly still didn't understand what had happened.

"I knew Geri in Waynesbridge," she told Thea. "From before my family moved to Shadyside."

"And you two never hit it off?" guessed Thea.

"Just the opposite," said Holly. "We met on the swim team. And even though we were the two best swimmers, we were never really rivals. It's hard to explain, but it was like if one of us won an event, it felt as if both of us had won."

"So what happened?" asked Thea.

Holly shook her head. "It was something really stupid," she said. "Geri and I had gotten to be good friends outside of school. We'd sleep over, hang out, do homework together. We were practically like sisters. And then she met this guy."

"Aha!" said Thea. "The plot thickens."

"Only it's not funny," said Holly, feeling again the pain of that time two years earlier. "His name was Brad Berlow, and he thought he was God's gift to the world. Only he was really a dork. Plus he was eighteen years old and had already graduated from high school. Naturally Geri's parents said she couldn't go out with him."

"If I know Geri, that didn't stop her," said Thea.

"She was convinced she was madly in love with Brad," said Holly. "She told me her life would be ruined if she didn't see him. Then she asked me to cover for her and say she was with me when she was with Brad."

"Nice," said Thea sarcastically. "So what did you do?"

"It turned into a mess," Holly admitted. "You know me. I'm not good at lying, but I promised her I wouldn't say anything about Brad to her parents. I just wasn't sure I could tell a direct lie. So Geri said she understood and basically everything was fine until one night about eleven o'clock her mother called my house looking for her."

"What did you tell her?"

"I was so rattled I just blurted out I hadn't seen Geri, so her mother goes, 'But she's supposed to be studying with you.' So like a dope I said, 'Oh, I forgot, she isn't here yet.'"

"At eleven o'clock at night?"

"Right," Holly agreed gloomily. "So now Mrs. Marcus is really upset and worried about Geri, so I start telling her I'm sure Geri's okay, and somehow she figured out that Geri was with Brad."

"Whoa," said Thea.

"So the next day Geri called. Her voice sounded so cold, I almost didn't recognize it. She said she was grounded for the rest of the semester, and it was all my fault. That I did it because I was jealous. I tried to explain what happened, but she wouldn't listen. She's hated me ever since."

Thea was silent a moment. "But it wasn't your fault," she said. "You told her you couldn't tell a lie! She should never have asked you to do it."

"But she did," said Holly. "And maybe if I'd been a better friend, I'd have found some way to keep her mother from getting suspicious."

"I doubt it," said Thea. "Anyway, it's all in the past now."

"I thought it was," said Holly. "When we moved to Shadyside, I thought I'd never have to worry about Geri again. But now she's *here.*"

"Just ignore her," said Thea sympathetically. "Don't let her ruin your summer."

"I'll try," said Holly doubtfully.

There was a sudden raucous burst of laughter from outside, followed by shouts and more laughter. "It looks like most of the rest of the counselors have arrived," said Thea. "Let's go check them out."

"Let's go look for John, you mean," teased Holly.

"Well, that too," said Thea. With a last look around the rec room, the girls stepped back out into the sunshine. It was late in the afternoon and beginning to cool a little. Across the parking lot three boys were taking turns hitting softballs, while a tall girl pitched for them. Automatically Holly looked around for

Geri, then saw that she was sitting at a picnic table with a book open in front of her. Across the table a handsome boy was frowning in concentration as he wrote something.

"I don't know everyone," Thea told Holly. Then she pointed straight up. "I could introduce you to Kit, but the clown is up in a tree," she said. Holly followed her friend's exasperated gaze to see a tall, gangly boy shinnying up to the top of a maple.

"Is he crazy, or what?" asked Holly.

"What," said Thea. *"And* crazy. Oh, look who's here."

The tall girl who'd been pitching crossed the parking lot with a friendly smile on her face.

"Hi, Thea," she said in a warm voice. "Is this Holly?" Holly watched the older girl approaching them. The girl's skin was darkly tanned, and her long, shiny black hair was twisted into two long braids. She was wearing a short one-piece jumpsuit of faded denim, and around her neck hung a beautiful jade pendant of an owl.

Holly just stared. She thought the girl was incredibly attractive. No. Holly thought she was perfect.

"I'm Debra Wallach," the girl said. "I'm senior counselor in your cabin." She stuck her hand out, and Holly shook it, suddenly nervous.

"I'm glad to meet you," Holly said. "I'm supposed to be your assistant."

"I know that," said Debra. "In arts and crafts and boating. Have you done this before? What experience have you had?"

"Uh, not much," admitted Holly, more rattled than

19

ever. "I mean, I've *done* a lot of crafts but never taught it. Them."

"I see," said Debra. Was Holly just imagining it, or had her voice become cool?

"I've had a lot of experience boating, though," Holly went on quickly. "I've gone sailing with my father every summer since I was three."

"Unfortunately, we don't have sailboats here," said Debra. "Just canoes and rowboats."

She thinks I'm a complete jerk, Holly thought gloomily.

"The important thing is to work hard and be willing to learn," Debra said, her voice friendly again. "As long as you remember that, we'll get along fine." She winked at Holly, then walked off toward the office.

"She's tough, isn't she?" said Holly.

"The toughest," said Thea. "But she can be really nice too—as long as you do things the way she wants them done."

"I'd better get back to my cabin and unpack the rest of my stuff," said Holly, suddenly worrying about what perfect Debra would think if she found Holly hadn't finished unpacking.

"I'll walk you," said Thea. "My cabin's right behind yours, and all my stuff is still sitting on my bunk."

As they approached the table where Geri was sitting with the good-looking boy, Geri raised her eyes to Holly with a face that was absolutely blank. Even a frown would have been better. What is she thinking? Holly wondered.

Thea apparently hadn't noticed and cheerfully

slapped the boy on the back. "Hi ya, Mick," she said. "Writing home already?"

Mick, who was tall and blond and looked like the actor Kevin Bacon, seemed to be embarrassed and covered the paper with his hand. "As a matter of fact, I am," he said. "My mom likes to hear from me a lot. So I write a bunch of letters at the beginning of the summer and then send one a week."

"How do you know what's going to happen?" Thea asked.

"I just make it up," said Mick. "Sort of like predicting. And if you don't leave me alone, I'll write that you got eaten by a bear!"

Thea laughed, then introduced Mick to Holly.

"Nice to meet you," said Mick. "I think I'll write my mom that you and I have gotten to be close—very close friends."

Holly just smiled at him, flustered. He was gorgeous, but there was something a little dangerous looking about him.

Forget Mick, she told herself. You're taking a vacation from boys this summer.

"See you later," she said as she and Thea continued down the path.

"You can count on it!" said Mick, grinning.

She was still thinking about him when she got to her cabin. "See you at the campfire," said Thea.

"Right," said Holly. Still thoughtful, she wandered into the cabin. Through the window she could see the orange sunlight slanting off the lake. It really is beautiful here, she thought. And so far, it was shaping up to be an interesting summer. She thought she was going to like working with Debra, Mick was intriguing, and Thea was her best friend in the world. If only Geri weren't there. But maybe, Holly thought, she could have a talk with Geri and explain the misunderstanding once and for all.

She retrieved her pillow from the nearby bunk and, after inspecting it for bugs, replaced it on her own bunk. Then she began to unpack her last bag, the little overnight bag with her sunscreen, toothbrush, and other cosmetics, and put away the stuff Thea had dumped.

As it got closer to sunset, the cabin became darker, and at a slight noise she tilted her head back to inspect the ceiling.

And froze.

There, indistinct against the dark shadows, a huge shape fluttered, then swooped down toward her.

chapter
5

*I*t zoomed right over her head.

Instinctively Holly shut her eyes and covered her head with her hands. When she finally opened her eyes, nothing was there.

Her heart was pounding so hard she felt as if it would pop out of her chest.

I just imagined I saw something, she told herself. It was only a shadow.

But then something fluttered at the edge of her vision, and turning toward it she recognized it: a bat.

An enormous brown bat.

Before she had time to move or think, the bat, its mouth open wide, again flew over her, just grazing her hair.

She jumped back with a scream and grabbed a towel from the top of her cubby. Frantically she beat at the creature, driving it back, up toward the ceiling.

I've got to get it out of here, she thought. I've got to make it leave.

She glanced wildly about the room for a more substantial weapon. She saw nothing. But then she noticed the canoe paddle leaning against the corner. Before the bat could swoop toward her again, she grabbed the paddle and began swinging it at the creature. Startled, the bat flew to the far side of the room, then began circling frantically.

Holly fought down her rising panic. Even more than snakes and bugs, she was afraid of bats! But she could see that the bat was afraid of her too.

Maybe, she thought, she could chase it outside with the paddle.

Her hands trembling, she raised the paddle and swung it at the bat. The animal's only response was to fly in even wider circles, emitting a frightened high-pitched squeal.

Holly gradually made her way to the back of the room, fighting her revulsion, and slowly waved the paddle in the air. The bat flew away from her to the front of the room.

It's working! Holly thought and continued to guide the bat toward the door.

And then suddenly, without warning, the bat turned and flew directly at her face.

Still clutching the paddle, and screaming involuntarily, Holly darted under the screaming creature and out the door—

Directly into Geri Marcus.

"Why don't you watch where you ⟶" Geri, jumping back. Then she saw the pad⟶ terror on Holly's face, and she smiled nastily. canoeing?" she asked.

Holly felt her face redden. To her embarrassment, she saw that Geri was not alone—with her were Debra and two other girls Holly hadn't met.

"What's going on?" Debra demanded.

"There's a bat," Holly gasped. "A big bat in my cabin."

"Ewwww!" said one of the new girls.

"Oh, for heaven's sake!" said Debra, sounding disgusted. "Why didn't you just chase it out? Someone go get a broom."

One of the girls went off to the main building while Holly started to explain that she had been trying to chase the bat out when it flew at her.

"What did you expect?" said Debra. "It was probably terrified." The other counselor returned with a broom, and Debra took it into the cabin. Holly couldn't make herself go back in, so she just stood and watched the door, feeling helpless and embarrassed.

"There are a lot of bats in these woods," Geri said. Holly heard the glee in her voice and couldn't think of an answer.

A moment later the bat flew out the front door toward the woods. Debra followed, holding the broom. "Come on, girls," she said, setting it down. "We're going to be late for the campfire."

Holly took a deep breath to force herself to calm down, then followed the others to the clearing near the

…nselors were already
…roaring fire in the early
…w Thea sitting by herself

…wn and spearing a hot dog

…ounded glum, and Holly was
…was wrong when Mick came
over a… …the two of them.

"Welcome … …first cookout of the season," he said, giving Holly a big smile.

"Everything smells delish," said Holly, smiling back.

"Try the potato salad," said Mick. "It's one of Uncle Bill's specialties. Too bad being on time isn't another one."

Holly smiled. Uncle Bill always ran late, because he tried to do too many things at once.

"So we're just hanging out till he shows up," Mick went on. "Too bad we don't have a video to watch."

"Great idea, Mick," said Thea. "I thought the whole point of camp was to get away from civilization."

"I wasn't thinking of civilized videos," countered Mick. "You know how people tell ghost stories around campfires? I was just thinking it'd be even better to watch horror videos."

"I don't like horror movies," said Holly.

"Really?" said Mick. "Not even the *Friday the Thirteenth* movies?"

"I never saw them," admitted Holly.

"I don't believe it!" said Mick. "Everyone's seen

Friday the Thirteenth movies. There are at least eight of them. You're kidding, right?"

"She's not," said Thea. "Holly really doesn't like movies much. She reads books instead."

"You don't know what you're missing," said Mick. "They're great. See, the whole thing is there's this weird guy who wears a hockey mask, and he goes around killing campers—"

"Gross!" said Holly.

"It's really exciting," Mick went on. "There's this one scene in the first movie where a camper goes out in the woods alone, and she doesn't know the guy with the hockey mask is there, and he's got this hatchet, see—"

"I get the picture," said Holly.

Mick laughed. "Well, I still think you should see it. I'll be back in a minute," he added. "I need to get some more potato salad."

Holly turned to Thea. "Do you really like those dumb horror movies?" she asked her friend.

"They're okay," said Thea. "Sometimes it can be fun to be scared." She smiled, then began smearing mustard on her hot-dog bun.

Fun to be scared . . . Holly looked at the trees looming at the edge of the campfire. Now that it was dark, the woods no longer appeared to be friendly and inviting, but instead seemed only to be full of dark, menacing shapes.

She scooted a little closer toward the warmth and cheerful light of the campfire. Directly across the fire she noticed Geri, who was chatting and laughing with some of the other junior counselors.

27

This whole thing was a mistake, she thought. How can I make it through a whole summer here?

A whistle suddenly blew and immediately cheered her up. It was Uncle Bill, carrying a huge cooler. "More sodas," he announced, setting the cooler down. "Plenty for everyone. Whatever you like."

Several of the counselors got up and helped themselves while Uncle Bill seated himself on a big rock at one side of the fire. He glanced at Holly and gave her a quick, private wink, then began talking again in his hearty, booming voice.

"I want to welcome all of you to Camp Nightwing," he said. "For the new counselors, my name is Bill Patterson, but everyone calls me Uncle Bill. The campers will be arriving tomorrow, so just remember to keep cool and have a good time. That's rule number one—have a good time. Rule number two is to follow all the other rules. You've all received a printed list, but I'll just hit the high spots—"

There was a sudden rustling in the woods behind Uncle Bill.

For a moment he stopped talking, then went on. "If you're new here, you might be a little nervous about the things you hear in the woods at night. But there's nothing to be afraid of. In fact, this camp is the healthiest, most wholesome place you could possibly spend your summer."

The rustling noise had started again, much louder now. All of the counselors were staring at the edge of the woods.

What could it be? Holly wondered. Were there

bears? She couldn't keep her mind on what Uncle Bill was saying.

"So before we go any further," he said, finally cutting into her thoughts, "I think we ought to introduce ourselves. I've already told you who I am, so let's just go around the circle. Debra?"

"My name is Debra Wallach," the dark-haired girl said. "This is my third year at camp. I'm a boating counselor, and I also work in arts and crafts."

The boy sitting next to her started to speak but stopped because of a bloodcurdling scream from the edge of the woods.

An instant later the brush parted, and a figure leaped forward into the firelight.

He was dressed in a dark shirt and pants, a hockey mask gleaming on his face.

As Holly watched, horrified, he pulled a hatchet out of his belt and began to advance on her.

chapter
_____

6

Holly stared, unable to speak, as the masked figure waved his hatchet.

Someone across the fire from her screamed, and then Uncle Bill's booming voice filled the air.

"Very funny, Kit," he said calmly. "Thanks for reminding us of my favorite film."

"Hey, man," said the masked figure. "Come on, admit it—I saw your face—you were just as scared as everyone else."

"Not scared," said Bill. "Horrified—at the thought of a whole summer of your idiotic jokes."

The others laughed, and Kit removed his mask, revealing a pale face with freckles and light blue eyes.

"For those who don't know him," said Uncle Bill,

"this deadly hatchet murderer is Kit Damon. Watch your step around him, and I mean that literally."

Thea leaned close to Holly. "Kit thinks his jokes are hilarious," she whispered. "But I think he's a little weird."

"A little weird?" whispered Holly.

"Last summer he really scared a couple of kids with one of his stunts," Thea went on. "Uncle Bill almost threw him out of camp. I can't believe he allowed him back this summer."

Holly didn't answer. Suddenly she felt worse for Uncle Bill than ever. She knew why he had to rehire Kit—he was desperate for staff.

A short, plump counselor across the fire was introducing herself, but Holly couldn't understand her because she mumbled. She noticed that Kit had plopped down next to Geri, but Geri was ignoring him.

"Kit's crazy about Geri," Thea whispered. "All last summer he followed her around like a puppy dog."

"She doesn't seem to be too thrilled with him," said Holly.

"She thinks he's a nerd," said Thea. "But he just doesn't give up. I think one reason he works so hard at his 'jokes' is to get her to notice him."

Mick had just finished introducing himself, and now a tall, handsome boy with sun-streaked blond hair began speaking.

"I'm Sandy Wayne," the boy said, "and I'm from Center City. I'll be teaching tennis and wilderness camping."

"He's new," Thea whispered. "I tried to talk to him this afternoon, but he didn't have anything to say."

"Maybe he's shy," said Holly.

"Maybe," agreed Thea. "I think he's got money. He was wearing those Porsche sunglasses. You know, the ones that cost two hundred dollars. What kind of person would wear two-hundred-dollar shades in a place like this?"

"A rich one. Next question," said Holly with a laugh.

"If he has so much money, then why is he working here?"

"Maybe he just likes the outdoors," said Holly, beginning to feel exasperated. Sometimes Thea's nosiness got to her.

"That's John," Thea said, pointing to the compact, dark, good-looking boy in cutoff jeans and a green rugby shirt who was introducing himself as John Hardesty. Holly noticed that he didn't meet anyone's eyes, and especially seemed to be avoiding Thea's.

"He's been sitting by himself all night," said Thea. "Tying knots in a rope. He hasn't come over to see me or even waved."

"Maybe he didn't see you," said Holly, aware of how lame that sounded even as she said it.

"Maybe," said Thea. "But I doubt it."

Now Holly understood why Thea had been so jumpy all evening. She tried to think of something comforting to say to Thea because it seemed as if John hadn't been as thrilled by last summer's romance as Thea had been.

The introductions were finally over, and Holly wondered if she'd ever be able to keep all the names straight.

"It's getting late now," Uncle Bill was saying, "so I won't keep you much longer. You've all got printouts of the camp rules.

"I just want to go over a few of the more important ones. Lights out is at nine o'clock sharp for the campers and at ten-thirty for the counselors."

There were two or three groans of protest, and Mick asked, "What about weekends or when we're off duty?"

"No exceptions," said Uncle Bill firmly. "Whenever I've made exceptions in the past, people overslept in the morning."

"Most of the rules aren't bad compared to those of other camps," Thea whispered to Holly. "But Uncle Bill is really strict about the ones he does have."

"We recycle soda cans and paper—you'll find the appropriate bins in the mess hall," Uncle Bill continued. "And finally—and this one is a biggie—counselors are absolutely forbidden to date campers. By date I mean hang out with socially, hold hands, go to the dances together . . . in other words, be involved with. If you see your true love among the campers, that's fine. See them during the school year. But not here. Not ever. Anyone who breaks this rule will immediately be expelled from camp. Any questions?"

"What if one of the campers falls madly in love with me?" said Kit. "What am I supposed to do then?"

"Call *Ripley's Believe It or Not*," joked Mick.

The others all laughed, and for a moment Holly felt a little sorry for Kit. So far his two jokes had backfired on him.

Uncle Bill signaled he was finished by standing and walking closer to the fire. "Don't stay up too late," he said with a friendly grin. "Remember we all start work tomorrow."

Holly watched affectionately as her uncle lumbered off. Some of the kids started roasting marshmallows, while others began drifting off to their cabins.

Holly suddenly became aware that she was very tired and decided to go to bed early.

"Walk back to the cabin with me?" she said to Thea.

Thea nodded. "Wait here," she said. "I'm going to say hi to John."

Holly watched as Thea crossed to the other side of the campfire, where John was still sitting by himself, staring blankly into the fire. She couldn't hear what he said when Thea approached, but her heart sank when she saw the cold, unemotional look on John's face. He was reacting to Thea like a zombie. What on earth did Thea see in him, anyway?

Holly watched as Thea gamely continued to talk. Just then someone grabbed Holly's arm from behind. She spun around to see Mick grinning at her.

"Ready for your first night in the woods?" he said. Up close he looked even more like Kevin Bacon.

"I think so," she said. "So far so good, anyway."

"If you get scared, just call on me," he said. "I'll protect you."

"Until lights out, anyway," she cracked.

"Or after. Don't let Uncle Bill scare you with his

rules. He talks like he's rough and tough, but he's a pussycat underneath."

Holly couldn't help smiling because she knew that what Mick said was true.

"Walk you back to your cabin?" Mick said then.

"Thanks anyway," said Holly. "I'm walking with Thea. We have some things to talk about."

"Another time, then," said Mick. "After all, it's a long summer." He turned and sauntered off. Holly watched him go, her heart beating fast. What was it about him that was so attractive? Was it that he seemed somehow . . . dangerous?

She turned back to find Thea and was startled to see Geri standing under a tree only a few feet away. Geri was staring directly at Holly with hatred so intense Holly could feel it move through her body. When Geri caught her eye, she didn't blink, but continued to glare angrily, even menacingly.

chapter
7

Dear Chief,

Things are off to a good start. I've started my work already, just as I promised you. It wasn't easy taking the bolts out of the wall, but it worked like a dream—or a nightmare. It's just too bad that the whole cabinet didn't come down. But I have plenty of time.

After all, lots of accidents can happen in a summer camp—lots of deadly accidents.

Please write and let me know how you are doing. Remember, Chief, I'm always here for you.

Yours forever,
Me

chapter
8

*H*olly was awakened before six by the songs of a thousand birds. Usually she liked to sleep as late as possible, but the golden sunlight and the fresh pine-scented air streaming in through the cabin window made her feel wide awake and refreshed.

Who knows? she thought to herself. Maybe I am an outdoors person and just never knew it.

Debra was still asleep in her bunk across the room, so Holly dressed quickly and quietly, slipping into her new pink-striped bathing suit and grabbing a towel before stepping outside.

A faint, hazy mist hung over the woods to the east, and the ground around the cabins was lightly dusted with dew. It's really beautiful here, she thought. No wonder Uncle Bill loves it so much.

She followed the path down to the lake, the pine needles tickling her bare feet.

She had nearly reached the shore when she heard a pounding noise behind her and realized that someone was running after her down the path.

Startled, she turned around quickly, then relaxed when she saw Sandy jogging toward her. He was dressed in a red warm-up suit and the fancy sunglasses Thea had mentioned.

"Hi," he said, slowing. "I hope I didn't startle you. I always go for a run in the morning."

"I hardly ever do *anything* in the morning," said Holly with a yawn. "But it's so beautiful today, I just couldn't resist a swim."

"I know what you mean," said Sandy. "Say—want to come for a walk in the woods? There's a birds' nest I found yesterday. The little birds are almost old enough to fly. They're really fun to watch."

"That sounds great," said Holly. "I'd like to see them later. But I don't have a lot of time this morning."

"Right," said Sandy, smiling. "But listen—be careful about swimming alone. The lake gets deep very suddenly. And stay away from the muddy bank. That's where the leeches are."

"Thanks," said Holly. "Leeches, yuck! I'll stay in the roped-off section."

"Then you'll be fine," said Sandy. "Have a nice swim." He turned onto another path and disappeared into the woods, the soft thud of his Nikes gradually fading.

Holly made a mental note to get to know Sandy better. He was good-looking and had a great smile. But for some reason there wasn't anything exciting about him, not like—

"Hi, there!" Holly was jolted out of her thoughts as Mick suddenly appeared on the path ahead of her.

"Oh!" she said, jumping. "Where did you come from?"

"The woods," said Mick. "Sorry if I scared you. I like to cut through the woods. It's more interesting than taking the marked path."

"I was just going to take a quick swim," said Holly.

"So I see," said Mick admiringly. He studied her so intently that Holly felt herself begin to blush.

"Nice suit," he said. Then he grinned. "Mind if I walk with you? I want to check out the boats before the campers get here."

"Sure," said Holly. "I'll help. I'm supposed to be assisting Debra in boating instruction."

"We have canoes and rowboats," Mick explained. "The kids all like the canoes best. Last year we had five, but there was a—an accident, so there are only four now."

The boat dock was just over a little hill that looked directly down into the lake. In the early-morning light the lake gleamed with golden streaks of reflected sunshine.

"The lake's so beautiful," Holly said. "Does it have a name?"

"Feather Lake," said Mick. "It got its name because of all the waterfowl that stop here on their migrating path. My grandfather grew up around here, and he once told me that—whoa!" He stopped talking suddenly and jogged the remaining few feet to the dock.

"What's the matter?" asked Holly, catching the note of alarm in his voice.

"The canoes—I see only one—"

Holly ran after him onto the short wooden dock. Bobbing at the ends of their leads were three rowboats and one battered-looking canoe.

"They're in the water!" said Mick. "Over here!"

Holly bent her head to see where he was pointing. Beneath the clear surface of the lake she could make out three canoes resting on the sandy bottom, each with a large hole in the side.

"How could that happen?" she asked.

"I don't know," said Mick. "But those holes weren't accidentally made." He took off his canvas hightops and jumped into the water, soaking his cutoffs and T-shirt. "Come on," he ordered. "Help me."

Holly dropped her towel and followed Mick into the chilly water. Together they began to push and pull at the canoe nearest the shore, finally getting it up onto the grassy bank. Mick tipped it onto its side to let the remaining water drain out, then squatted to study the hole.

"Someone must have punched it in," he said, pointing to the jagged aluminum edges. "Maybe with a chisel."

Holly touched the sharp edge around the hole, then saw something that made the hair on the back of her neck prickle. Just beside the hole, stuck between a seat of the canoe and the gunwale, was a soggy red feather.

By the time Holly and Mick finished pulling the other two canoes out of the water, it was midmorning. The canoes were heavy, and Holly's muscles ached. She had missed breakfast, but there was no time to eat. She only had time to get to her cabin, change, and rush to meet the arriving campers.

On the way back to her cabin and while she changed, Holly thought about what had happened. She inspected the soggy red feather and put it next to the one from the rec room in her top dresser drawer. Was the second feather a coincidence? Or had someone deliberately unbolted the cabinet and slashed the canoes and left the feathers as—what? Warnings?

"Holly, hurry up!" It was Thea at the door. "Debra's been asking where you are. The first bus just arrived!"

Holly forgot about the feathers and hurried out of the cabin after her friend. The big paved parking lot was crowded with counselors and campers.

Debra, her dark braids wound around her head like a crown, was checking names off on a clipboard as the campers climbed out of the bus.

"Debra, I'm sorry," Holly began to apologize. "Some of the canoes were sunk, and I've been helping Mick—"

"I don't have time for excuses," said Debra brusquely. She thrust a list at Holly. "These are the six girls in Cabin Five," she said. "Round them up and help them get settled in. I have to go to check on a delivery at the crafts tent. I'll meet you back at the cabin in a few minutes."

Holly took the list, feeling stung. Debra hadn't even wanted to listen to her. Then she looked at the list with misgivings. There were dozens of campers—girls, boys, young ones, older ones—milling around the parking lot. How would she ever find the ones who belonged to Cabin Five?

"Just call out their names," said a familiar voice. Holly looked up gratefully to see a smiling Uncle Bill. "Don't worry, Holly," he said. "Nobody knows who the new campers are at first."

Feeling much better, Holly began reading the list of names aloud, and miraculously soon found all six campers. The girls were so excited to be at camp that Holly caught their enthusiasm, and by the time they reached the cabin, she'd forgotten all the unpleasantness earlier that morning.

The six girls were to share three bunk beds on one wall of the cabin. Two girls, twin sisters named Stacey and Suzie, immediately picked the bunk beds nearest the door. Candy and Melissa, who were apparently good friends, picked the middle bunk. But the two remaining girls, Jessica and Tracy, immediately began arguing over the third one.

"I get the top!" Tracy declared.

"No, I get it," said Jessica. "My mom told me I'd get to sleep in a top bunk at camp!"

"That's not fair!" said Tracy. "I saw it first!" She had already put her pack on the bunk and was pointing at it smugly.

"I have an idea, girls," said Holly. "Why don't you

take turns with the top bunk? The first week one of you can have it, and the next week the other one."

"Okay," said Tracy, "but I get it first!"

"No, *me!*" protested Jessica, her eyes welling up with tears.

"Why don't you let Tracy have it this week?" said Holly gently. "She already has her things on it."

"It's not fair," mumbled Jessica. But Holly could see that the girl had already become interested in something she could see outside the window. "Oh, look!" she said. "They're playing dodgeball!"

"Well, hurry and get unpacked and we'll all go out to play," said Holly, relieved. She turned to help Candy, who was the smallest camper, get her bulky suitcase open.

This is going to be all right, she thought. The girls are darling, and when Debra gets back, we ought to be able to handle them easily.

She had just managed to unlock the suitcase when there was a strange creaking noise behind her, and then an ear-splitting crash.

chapter
9

Holly spun around and saw to her horror that the top bunk of Tracy and Jessica's bed had collapsed onto the bottom one. Beneath a pile of bedding she could just see a little white arm sticking out.

She ran toward the bunk, ignoring the screams of the other girls, and pulled away the tangled mass of blankets and sheets. "Tracy!" she called. "Tracy! Are you all right?"

She gave a sigh of relief as Tracy, on top of the collapsed bed, raised her eyes to her with a dazed expression and then began to sob.

"There, there," Holly said. "It's all right now." She helped the girl off the jumbled heap, then turned to

Jessica, who was standing beside the bed, wailing. "What happened?" she asked.

"I don't know!" Jessica bawled.

"I climbed up on the bunk," blubbered Tracy. "It fell down."

"But—but how? Did you pull on anything?" Holly tried to hide her exasperation.

"I didn't do anything!" cried Tracy, and she began to sob even louder.

"I didn't mean you did," said Holly. "I was only trying to find out—" But she gave up. It was obvious that both girls were too upset to talk about what had happened. She put her arms around Tracy and began to rub her back to comfort her.

Just then she heard a bang as the cabin door was flung open. Standing in the doorway was Debra, her face white with anger.

"What have you done?!" Debra shouted. She quickly crossed the room and scooped up Tracy. "What's the matter, honey?" she crooned to the little girl. "Did Holly scare you?"

"I didn't do anything!" protested Holly, stung. "The bunk collapsed! I was trying to comfort the girls!"

"You call this comfort?" said Debra sarcastically, gesturing about the room, where the six girls were all crying.

"They were scared," said Holly. "We all were. It made a lot of noise—"

"Hey, Debra!" called a voice from the doorway. "What's happening?" Holly turned and saw with a sinking feeling that it was Geri, along with another of the junior counselors.

"What does it look like?" shouted Debra above the sounds of sobbing. "Holly had some sort of accident while the girls were getting unpacked."

"I did not!" cried Holly. "I didn't have anything to do with it! Tracy climbed—"

But her explanation was cut off by Uncle Bill's booming voice. "What's going on here?" he demanded. "I heard all the commotion clear down at the rec room."

"One of the bunks collapsed," said Debra.

"Collapsed?" said Uncle Bill. "How?"

"I don't know," said Debra. "Apparently, it happened when one of the girls climbed on it."

Uncle Bill walked over and inspected the bed. "I don't understand," he mused. He straightened up and dusted his hands off on his khaki shorts. "Well," he said, "I'll send the handyman over to fix this and to inspect all the other beds. Thanks for your quick thinking, Debra."

As he strode out of the cabin, Holly stared after him, speechless. Debra hadn't done anything except make things worse by screaming at her.

"Well, don't just stand there!" Debra snapped. "You've got to help the girls!"

Once again Holly felt her cheeks grow red. What did Debra think she was doing? As she turned to comfort Jessica, who was still crying, she saw that Geri was in the cabin now, a strange triumphant smile on her face.

"There, there, Jessica," Holly said, picking up the little girl. "Don't cry. It's all right." She sat on the

46

bunk next to the one that had collapsed and continued to soothe Jessica, finding her words strangely soothing to herself too. Jessica's sobs had diminished to intermittent quiet little gasps, so Holly focused her attention on the collapsed bed. One of the slats had broken and was poking up with sharp splinters protruding. Idly she flipped over the slat to pull out the longest splinter, then froze.

Taped to the underside of the slat was a red feather.

For a long moment Holly just stared at the feather. I don't believe this is still only the morning of the first day of camp, she thought. What's going to happen next? She took a deep breath to calm down, then stood up ready to help the young campers unpack.

Out in the main yard Sandy and another counselor were leading team games.

Holly took her girls to join them, but she couldn't get her mind to focus on anything but the red feather.

That made three red feathers.

They seemed to add up to only one thing: Someone was deliberately trying to destroy the camp.

And then another thought formed in her mind. She had found the feathers. All three. Why? Was their message meant for *her?*

"I've got to take care of something," she told Sandy, making a sudden decision. "If anyone wants me, I'll be in Uncle Bill's office."

"Sure thing," said Sandy, flashing his friendly grin.

Her heart pounding, Holly knocked on Uncle Bill's door. At his mumbled "Come in," she pushed it open. He was hunched over his battered wooden desk. A worried frown creased his forehead when he first raised his head, but when he saw who it was, he smiled his familiar, hearty smile. "Well, hi, there, Prin— Holly," he said. "I wish I had some time to sit and shoot the breeze with you, but I've got to finish these accounts and then see about getting that bunk and the canoes fixed."

"That's what I want to talk to you about," said Holly. "The bunk bed and the canoes. Uncle Bill, I'm positive that—"

"I'm sorry, Holly," he cut in. "I really don't have any time right now."

"But this is important!" she protested.

"I'm sure it is," he said, and she recognized his no-nonsense voice. He was about one step from getting mad. "Everything that demands my attention is important. But first things just have to come first."

"But—"

"I mean it, Holly!" he said, the frown back. "I'll talk to you when I have time. Please close my door on your way out."

Holly left the office feeling more frustrated than ever. If he didn't have time now, and camp was just beginning, when would he have time? And how was she going to warn him of the danger?

A glance at her watch told her it was almost time for lunch, and she cheered up for the first time all day. She hadn't eaten breakfast and she was starving. Delicious smells were coming from the mess hall. As she hurried up the path toward the big building, she saw Debra standing alone under a tree.

On impulse Holly stepped off the path and joined her. "Hi," she said brightly.

"Hi," said Debra. There was no smile of welcome, just wariness in her dark eyes. She tossed her head impatiently, and the little jade owl on the thong around her neck bounced against her peach-colored T-shirt.

Holly took a deep breath. "I just want to say I'm sorry for what happened this morning," she said. "I don't know how things got so out of hand, but I promise I'll try harder from now on."

"Let's hope so," said Debra.

"But I also want to ask you something . . . something that will make it easier for me to do my job." She paused a moment. When Debra didn't answer, she went on as calmly as she could. "I—I felt really bad when you scolded me in front of the girls and the other counselors," she said. "I'd really appreciate it if you wouldn't do that again. If I do something you don't like, please, just tell me in private."

For a moment Debra just stared blankly at her, the expression in her eyes unreadable.

And then the expression became clear. It was anger.

"In other words," said Debra, "you want me to ignore emergencies so I won't hurt your feelings?"

"That's not what I said!" protested Holly.

"I had no choice but to speak to you this morning!" Debra went on, her voice rising. "I left you alone for five minutes, and we nearly had a hurt child on our hands. If I hadn't intervened, you'd probably still be standing there like a statue!"

"But all I—"

"Forget it, Holly!" Debra shouted over her protest. "The most important thing as far as I'm concerned is

49

the campers. Don't think you'll get special treatment just because you're Uncle Bill's niece!"

Holly started to answer, then shut her mouth. It was no use. Debra—and probably everyone else—knew she was related to Uncle Bill. How did she find out?

Holly turned to go into the mess hall and saw Geri standing at the entrance, obviously listening to—and enjoying—her argument with Debra.

Geri must have told Debra, Holly suddenly realized. Geri knew Uncle Bill from Waynesbridge. And, of course, she wouldn't pass up an opportunity to cause Holly trouble.

Geri turned away after making sure Holly saw the smile on her face, and Holly followed her into the mess hall, her appetite suddenly gone. As she got in the food line, Thea came up and took her arm. "Holly, what's wrong?" she said. "You look so upset."

"Everything's wrong," said Holly. "I don't want to talk about it."

"Listen," Thea went on, "I just found out something that will help explain a lot. Meet me by the lake tonight after the campers are in bed."

"Okay," Holly agreed. She didn't know what Thea had found out and didn't much care. At this point she didn't see how anything could help.

She filled her tray with a big spinach salad and a turkey sandwich, then went to join the campers from Cabin Five. She sat down opposite Debra, who barely acknowledged her. But as soon as Holly saw the girls, her mood improved. They were obviously happy to be with her and began to talk all at once, telling her about the wonderful time they'd had playing ball.

"Melissa won three points for our side," Tracy explained happily.

"Well, that's wonderful," said Holly. "I'll be sure to watch the next time you play."

"We'll be going swimming right after lunch," Debra told the girls and got up to get some coffee. "So don't eat too much."

"Don't worry, Debra, we won't," said Tracy. "We don't want to sink!"

Holly couldn't help laughing. The girls were all so darling.

Her appetite had returned, and she was just about to bite into the turkey sandwich when Kit came running into the mess hall, screaming in terror.

"Help! Somebody help!"

A monstrous green snake was wrapped around his arm.

The mess hall erupted into pandemonium, with the sounds of chairs scraping along the floor and falling over, and campers' screams drowning out Kit's cries for help.

"Help me!" Kit screamed again, struggling with the huge, writhing creature. "Please, won't someone help!"

His struggles had brought him closer to the Cabin Five table, and all at once he pulled the enormous snake off his arm—

And tossed it into the center of the table.

chapter
10

*H*olly just stared at the huge snake, unable to move.

All around her she could hear the screams of terrified campers as they scrambled to get away from the table.

Do something, Holly! she told herself.

But she could do nothing except stare at the snake.

As if in slow motion she watched as Thea ran over to her table, reached down, and—incredibly—picked up the snake to fling it against the wall of the mess hall.

Slowly Holly felt herself return to normal. Her heart slowed and her legs stopped trembling.

Then she became aware of a ripple of laughter that

quickly built to a roar. "It's rubber!" someone shouted, laughing. "The snake is rubber!"

One of the boy campers came over to the table holding the "snake" in his hand.

Now Holly could see that it was, in fact, just a rubber snake, not even that lifelike looking. Once again she felt her face grow hot with embarrassment.

Some of the Cabin Five campers were still crying in fright. "For heaven's sake, Holly!" said Debra, returning to the table. "It's bad enough you were scared by a rubber snake! Are you just going to sit there while the girls need help?"

With Thea's help Holly quickly began calming and soothing the younger girls.

"Don't feel bad. Everyone thought it was real," Thea whispered to Holly.

"Right," said Holly. "Thanks."

"Don't forget about tonight," Thea added. "Down by the lake." She returned to her own table, and Holly went back to her lunch. But she didn't feel like finishing it. She saw that Debra was giving her a disapproving look. "Debra," she said, knowing it would do no good, "I'm sorry. It's just that my whole life I've been scared of snakes. You see—"

"If you're so afraid of snakes," interrupted Debra, "then what are you doing at Camp Nightwing?"

Good question, Holly thought.

The rest of the day went well, and the campers were enjoying themselves so much that Holly forgot about her troubles.

Debra went to bed early, and Holly listened for the sound of her soft snoring before tiptoeing out of the cabin. In the silence of night she could hear a million crickets chirping, and the sky was so thick with stars that their light cast shadows.

Feeling a little scared and also a little thrilled, Holly began to pick her way down the path to the lake. Thea met her partway there.

"I guess you had a pretty bad introduction to camp," her friend said sympathetically.

"I guess it could have been worse," said Holly. "But I don't know how."

"Well," Thea went on, "I found something out this morning that might explain some of the grief you've been getting. I didn't realize it last year because of the difference in their ages, but Debra and Geri are good friends."

"Oh, no!" said Holly. "Well, that explains why Debra doesn't like me. Geri has probably poisoned her mind against me."

"Something like that," agreed Thea. "I couldn't believe how mad Debra got when you were scared of the snake. She thought it was real the same as everyone else."

"What I can't figure out," said Holly, "is why Kit threw it on *my* table. How did he know I'm afraid of snakes?"

"Maybe he didn't," said Thea. "But I'll bet Geri had something to do with it."

"Like maybe she just told Kit to do something to embarrass me," said Holly glumly.

"And of course whatever Geri wants, Geri gets,"

said Thea. They had reached the lake, and Thea sat on the edge of the dock, dangling her feet in the water. Holly sat next to her, leaning against one of the wooden supports. She watched as the moon rose over the lake, sending its silvery reflection into the rippling water.

"You know," Thea went on, "even if Geri didn't have a grudge against you, she might see you as a threat. She was Miss Popularity at camp last year. She even had a thing going with Mick."

Oh, no, thought Holly. Just one more reason for Geri to be against me.

She hugged her knees, trying to think of what to do, when there was a sudden howling in the distance.

"What was that?" cried Holly, jumping.

Thea shrugged. "A wolf, maybe," she said. "Don't they howl when the moon's out?"

"What am I doing here?" Holly suddenly wailed. "I don't like the outdoors, I'm scared of bugs and snakes, and half the counselors hate me! And now I have to listen to a wolf!"

"Lighten up. It's probably just a dog," said Thea. "Listen. I still think that if you give it a chance, you'll have a good time here this summer. But maybe—if you really feel bad—you ought to just give up and go home. I'm sure Uncle Bill would understand."

"That's the whole problem," said Holly. "He probably *would* understand. But he needs my help. Especially now that someone's trying to destroy the camp."

"What are you talking about?" said Thea.

"Remember the red feather we found in the rec

room yesterday?" Thea nodded. "Well," Holly went on, "there was another red feather in one of the broken canoes. And another one taped—*taped*—to the broken bunk bed in Cabin Five."

"That's weird," said Thea.

"It's more than weird," said Holly. "It's proof that the same person is responsible for all three so-called accidents. And what's really got me spooked is that the latest one was in *my* cabin."

"But why would anyone want to do those things?" asked Thea. Her voice was distracted, and Holly noticed that she kept glancing in the direction of the boys' cabins.

"I don't know why," Holly said. "And I don't mean to be paranoid. But I think it has something to do with me. I have to find out. Uncle Bill won't listen to me. I'm really glad to have you to talk to about it."

"What?" said Thea.

"I said I'm really glad— Thea, is something wrong?"

"I'm sorry," said her friend. "I guess I'm a little nervous. I asked John to meet me here tonight, but he doesn't seem to be showing up."

"Well, maybe he'll come later," Holly said.

"I don't know," said Thea. "It's really getting late." She sighed. "You know, I was so excited about seeing him again this summer. But he's been acting so strange ever since camp started. I can't figure out what's going on with him."

Holly just shrugged. She thought it was obvious that John just didn't care for Thea the way she did for him.

She yawned and stretched. "I'm beat," she said. "Want to go back to the cabins?"

Thea shook her head, a sad smile on her face. "I think I'll wait a few more minutes. He still might come."

"Okay," said Holly. "And thanks for what you told me about Debra. It doesn't make her attitude any easier to take, but at least I understand where she's coming from now."

She walked along the dock, then onto the path, feeling the chill of the night air. Somewhere an owl hooted, and Holly thought that given time she could really learn to love it out here.

She had passed the part of the path closest to the woods when there was a sudden crackling noise behind her.

It's just a leaf, she told herself.

The crackling repeated, and then again.

Footsteps.

Her heart pounding, she began to walk faster.

The footsteps began to move faster too.

Who—or what—could it be?

Holly turned around, but she saw nothing but trees and shadows.

I'm just imagining things, she told herself.

She stopped.

The footsteps stopped, then all at once they started again, faster, running.

Who could be in the woods at that time of night? Whoever it was was just behind her and getting closer.

chapter
11

*H*olly began walking faster.

The footsteps sped up too.

Then she heard voices. "It's this way," a girl said.

And another: "Come on, Cyndi! You heard what Uncle Bill said about lights out."

Holly let out a sigh of relief.

It was just two of the older girl campers, out late, trying not to get caught. She recognized them. The pretty blond one was named Courtney Blair. The other one was named Cyndi something.

Holly let a little smile form at the corner of her mouth, then stepped off the path into the woods.

"All right," she said. "It's pretty late to be out in the woods, isn't it?"

"We didn't mean anything," said Cyndi. "We were just going back to our cabin."

"Which cabin is that?" asked Holly, sounding as authoritative as she could.

"Eleven, on the other side of the main building," said Courtney.

"Well, I'll follow along and make sure you get there safe," said Holly. The girls hurried off again as if she'd shouted "Boo!" at them.

It's not so bad being a counselor, she thought. She liked the sense of responsibility.

She continued to follow them through the woods to make sure they really went to Cabin Eleven. They had come even with the main building when she saw a light off to one side of the path, and then she found herself staring into the light. She blinked, then squinted and saw that the flashlight was being held by Mick.

"Hi, Holly," he said. They were two simple words, but somehow the way he said them made her feel as if he knew everything about her.

"Hi, Mick," she said nervously. "What are you doing up so late?"

"Would you believe searching for you?" he said with a devilish smile.

"No," she said after a moment. "I wouldn't believe that."

"Well, I've found you, though," he said. "I've been wanting to talk to you all day. I never had a chance to thank you for helping me with the canoes."

"That's all right," she said. "I'm just glad no worse damage was done."

"I like the way you work," he went on. "Just helping me out, not asking a lot of questions and making excuses the way some girls would."

"Well, it was no big deal," Holly said.

"You're okay," Mick said. "I knew as soon as I met you that I wanted to get to know you better."

For a moment Holly didn't answer. She studied his face and saw that he was acting serious. Too serious. Why was he coming on so strong?

"I'm sure," she said carefully, "that we'll get to know each other better before the summer is over."

"I wanted to start now," he said. "Why don't you come for a walk with me?"

"Now?" she asked. "It's practically the middle of the night."

"That makes it even nicer," said Mick. In the darkness of the woods he looked so handsome, so mysterious, and Holly wondered how she had possibly gotten herself into this.

"I—I can't go for a walk with you now," she said. "I need to make sure that those girls got back to their cabin."

"Then afterward," said Mick. "I'll help you take them."

Holly realized she had made a mistake. When someone was as intense as Mick, you didn't just make excuses. You told the truth. She took a deep breath. "Not tonight, Mick," she said. "It's late, and lights out for counselors is in a few minutes."

"What's the matter?" asked Mick, his tone suddenly challenging. "Are you afraid to be alone with me?"

"Of course not," said Holly. "It's what I told you. I

60

want to check to make sure those girls got to their cabin, and then go to bed myself. It's been a long day."

"Yeah, sure," said Mick. He sounded angry and hurt. "You got a boyfriend back home? Is that it?"

"That doesn't have anything to do with it," said Holly, carefully not answering his question. "Now, please, Mick. Go on back to your cabin. I'll talk to you tomorrow."

"Maybe you'll talk to me tonight," Mick said, his voice rougher. Impulsively he grabbed her arm, and for a moment Holly felt afraid of him.

"Let go of me!" she exclaimed.

"I said—" Then he abruptly let go and turned away, almost disgusted. "Ah, what's the use?" he said. Without another word he stomped off through the woods.

What in the world was *that* about? Holly wondered. On one level she was flattered that someone as good-looking as Mick was so obviously interested in her. And she had to admit that she was attracted to him—more than she wanted to be.

But on another level she found Mick's attention frightening. Does everybody go crazy when they get out in the woods? she wondered.

By then she had checked to make sure the girls were in Cabin Eleven and told them good night. She started back down the path to Cabin Five.

She tried to relax, to listen to the crickets and the calls of the owls, but her mind was churning with a hundred thoughts, and her body felt as tight as a bow string. Well, she told herself, no wonder. I've got a lot to be nervous about.

As Cabin Five appeared, she at last felt herself relax.

Finally, she thought, and began to hurry down the path.

But then abruptly she stopped.

Was she imagining it? Or was someone sneaking out the door of Cabin Five?

Someone dressed in dark colors, moving stealthily.

She blinked hard, and the figure disappeared.

In its place she saw only shadows, shadows from the tall oak to the side of the cabin.

I imagined it, she told herself.

Or did I?

Confused, she stood still and surveyed the area. There was no sign of anyone. Everyone in camp— except her—was probably sound asleep.

A moment later she felt a tap on her shoulder.

She gave a little shriek and spun around in fright and anger. If it was Mick—

"Hey, take it easy," said a gentle voice. "I'm sorry. I didn't mean to startle you."

It was Sandy, his fair hair made even paler by the moonlight.

"Sandy!" Holly said, surprised and relieved. "What are you doing here?"

"Just taking a little stroll," he said, an odd expression on his face. "I always do that before lights out. Why do you ask?"

"I thought I saw someone coming out of my cabin," Holly blurted out.

"Do you think I was in your cabin?" Sandy acted shocked.

"I just thought you might have seen someone," Holly said.

"No," he said. "I didn't see anyone. No one." He had that odd expression again. "You're imagining things, Holly."

"Probably," said Holly. "This day has been one disaster after another."

"I know," he said sympathetically. "I saw the way Debra yelled at you this morning."

"I just can't seem to do anything right where she's concerned," said Holly.

"Don't let Debra upset you," Sandy said after a moment. "I think she's a perfectionist. She probably doesn't realize that you're doing the best you can."

"You're right, I am," said Holly. "Thanks for saying so."

"Hey," said Sandy, "I know what it's like to be alone in a strange place."

"This is your first year too, isn't it?" said Holly.

"My first year here," said Sandy. "Not my first year as a camp counselor. Last summer I was a counselor at a camp out west—in the desert."

"I never did this before," Holly said. "A few years ago my big sister did work in a camp."

"Are you and your sister close?" asked Sandy.

"Not really," said Holly. "She's almost ten years older."

"Well, all the same you're lucky to have her," he said. "I don't have any sisters or brothers." He sounded so sad when he said it that for a moment Holly felt sorry for him.

"Well, you'd better go on in," he said, sounding cheerful again.

"Thanks, Sandy," she said, meaning it. "You've restored my faith in human nature or something."

"Good," he said. "See you tomorrow." With a wave and a smile he walked off.

She tiptoed into the cabin and quickly but quietly began to get ready for bed.

I'm going to sleep like a rock tonight, she thought, turning down her blanket. She slid in between the cool sheets, laid her head on the pillow, then slipped her hand under the pillow the way she always did before falling asleep.

And felt something soft and smooth wriggle through her fingers.

With a shriek Holly jumped out of bed and threw her pillow across the room.

There, where the pillow had been, slowly uncoiling, was a green and white snake.

chapter
12

*F*or a brief moment Holly hoped that this too would turn out to be a rubber snake.

But, no. As she watched, trembling all over, its black forked tongue flicked in and out of its mouth.

The snake slithered under her covers.

Holly felt sick.

She tugged at the blanket—and saw the snake uncoil its dark body in bold relief against her white sheets. She screamed.

"What is it?" someone shouted, switching on the light.

"A snake!" Jessica's high voice sounded on the edge of panic.

"Kill it! Kill it!" cried Tracy.

"Look out! It's going to bite!" Stacey was standing on the top of her bunk, her little face white with terror.

"What is it this time?" Holly heard Debra's disgusted voice as the older counselor came over to her bunk, rubbing sleep from her eyes. On the other side of the room all the girls were screaming in confusion and terror.

"It's a . . . a snake," said Holly, trying not to sound hysterical. "There. It was under my pillow."

"That?" said Debra scornfully. "It's only a garter snake. For heaven's sake, Holly, what's the matter with you?"

As Holly watched, horrified and ashamed, Debra reached down and scooped the snake up in her hand, then opened the cabin door and tossed it out into the night.

All the girls were crying now, as frightened by the snake as Holly had been.

Debra just glared at Holly. "Do something!" she hissed. "You're worse than useless!"

Her cheeks stinging, Holly went to the girls in the nearest bunk, murmuring soothing words to them. One by one she helped each girl search through her bedclothes for proof that there were no more snakes.

After what seemed like hours, the girls calmed down. Soon the cabin was quiet and dark as everyone slept.

Everyone but Holly.

Her mind was a volcano—feelings of outrage, humiliation, and fear bubbled, ready to erupt.

That snake did not crawl under my pillow accidentally, she thought. But who put it there? Kit? Debra?
Geri?

I was lucky this time, she thought. It was just a
harmless snake.

But what about next time?

Stop it, Holly, she told herself. You're getting paranoid. Why would anyone want to hurt you?

It didn't make any sense.

Maybe Uncle Bill could figure it out.

Somehow, she had to make him listen to her.

"Tell them I ordered those supplies a month ago for
delivery this week!"

Uncle Bill's booming voice could be heard through-
out the main building where his office was, and he
didn't sound happy. "I don't care what caused the
mix-up!" he yelled. "I want those things delivered by
tomorrow at the latest, or you'll hear from my law-
yer!"

Holly waited until her uncle stopped shouting, then
nervously knocked on his door.

"Come in!" he snapped, then changed expressions
when he saw who it was. "Sorry," he said. "Having a
little hassle with one of my suppliers. Sometimes you
have to yell a little to keep them honest."

"Uncle Bill," Holly said, "I know how busy you are,
but I really need to talk to you for a few minutes. It's
important."

Bill set the papers he'd been holding down on the
desk. "Okay, Princess," he said. "I can spare a minute

for you. Even though I do have a hundred and one things to do before noon."

Holly took a deep breath, reached into her pocket, and withdrew the three red feathers she had saved. "See these?" she said.

"Red feathers," said Uncle Bill. "Yeah. So?"

"I found one of them in the hole where one of those bolts pulled out of the wall," Holly said. "I found the second one in one of the sunken canoes. And the third was taped to the bunk bed that collapsed."

"So?" repeated Uncle Bill.

"It proves that the three things were connected," Holly said. "That they weren't accidents."

Bill studied the feathers for a long moment, then he smiled gently. "It doesn't prove any such thing," he said. "But I can see how you might think so."

"But it does!" Holly protested. "How could those feathers get in those places unless someone put them there?"

Bill shook his head. "I want to show you something," he said. He led Holly over to the window and pointed to the bottom of the screen. There were several feathers stuck there—though none of them was red. "There are feathers all over this camp," he said. "Feathers from birds, feathers from the crafts cabin. I'd say finding three red feathers—or even a hundred red feathers—doesn't prove a thing except that you're at Camp Nightwing."

"But—"

"No *buts,* honey," he went on. "Now, I know how upsetting those accidents were to you. And I know some of the other counselors have been giving you a hard time. But that's no reason to let your imagination run away with you."

"I'm not imagining anything!" said Holly, suddenly angry. "I'm worried about you—and about the camp! What if I'm right? What if someone is trying to destroy it?"

Uncle Bill laughed without humor. "There's no reason in the world for anyone to want to do that," he said. "My own bad luck alone is probably enough to do me in."

"But I'm telling you it's not luck—those so-called accidents were—"

"Not related," he said, finishing her sentence. "But no matter how bad my luck has been, it's got to turn sometime. And I have a good feeling about this summer, Holly. I really think we're going to do it—make the camp a success. Now, can I count on your support?"

"Of course you can," she said.

"So you just stop worrying about feathers and concentrate on being the best counselor you can be. And don't be so sensitive. Remember the other counselors all mean well."

"Right," said Holly. She opened her mouth to try one more time to convince her uncle, but he was already on the phone, punching in numbers. He winked at her, then began speaking to someone named Hal.

Holly left the office more discouraged than ever. What Uncle Bill had told her about feathers being all over the camp didn't convince her.

Almost, but not quite.

Because, deep inside, she knew that she was right. Knew that someone was trying to ruin the camp, to ruin Uncle Bill. He was just too trusting to see it.

But he was right about one thing. She had to stop being so sensitive, to stop worrying about Geri and Debra.

Instead, she had to save her energy for keeping her eyes and ears open. No matter how hard she tried to avoid the thought, it kept coming back.

The camp was in great danger.

And so was she.

[...] Nightwing and relax and let your friends, the counselors, live their lives without getting on your case [...] alike.

Yours forever,

chapter
13

Camp Nightwing

Dear Chief,

I haven't heard from you in a long time now. A lot of things have been happening. Bad things. But they're also good, if you know what I mean.

I've been doing everything I promised and more. Now I'm ready to take the next step. The big step.

Someone in this camp is going to die.

I promised, and I'm going to deliver.

Very soon.

It will be the person who most deserves it. Too bad. She's kind of cute.

71

I'll write and tell you all about it. Please write back, Chief. I've been waiting so long for a letter.

Yours forever,
Me

chapter

14

H olly felt better. Scared. But better. She had decided what to do. She was going to find out what was happening in the camp. Uncle Bill wasn't going to do it.

So it had to be up to her.

Who could be doing these terrible things?

It had to be someone who was at camp all the time, since the incidents had happened at all hours.

And it had to be someone big and strong enough to sink the canoes and unscrew the cabinet bolts, which ruled out the campers, since they hadn't been there yet.

It had to be one of the counselors.

But which one?

She thought back to all the mystery shows she'd

seen on television. One of the first things the detectives always did was get to know as much as possible about the suspects.

So what she had to do was clear—she had to get to know the other counselors as well as she could. She had a perfect opportunity to observe the counselors that afternoon. There was a big softball game between Nightwing and another camp. The whole camp, including all the counselors, were to gather at the big field to cheer on the older Nightwingers as they took on a team from Camp Starlight.

The Starlight kids were tough. By the third inning they were ahead by seven runs, and the Nightwing campers were starting to lose interest.

Holly's group sat working on lanyards during the game and paid very little attention to the action on the field.

Holly's attention was on the counselors, particularly the counselors with whom she had had the most contact.

Kit, she noticed, always did as little work as possible while trying to seem busy. She laughed as she watched him spend ten minutes getting the first-aid kit "in order" while he was really using the time to try to get close to Geri.

John Hardesty worked hard. He was completely focused on the game and the campers. He practically ignored the other counselors—only speaking to them when he had to.

Sandy was like John, always working hard and keeping to himself. He seemed shy and hardly spoke to anyone but Holly. But during the game she saw him talking to Debra. Flirting? She'd never seen them talk together before.

Geri was one of the coaches. Even Holly had to admit that Geri really knew what she was doing. She expected a lot from the campers, but they liked her for it. And Mick . . . Mick was different. He was a good worker, but his mind always seemed to be somewhere else.

Holly watched and listened all day. When the game was over (final score 16 to 4), she helped lead Camp Nightwing in a cheer for Starlight and then took everyone down to the lake for a much-needed general swim. As she sat on the dock, waiting for the whistle that meant general swim was over, she had to admit the truth—none of the counselors ever said or did anything that seemed remotely suspicious. She was getting nowhere.

She had just finished collecting her campers' beach towels when Mick suddenly appeared beside her.

"Hi ya," he said.

"Hi, Mick," she said.

"So, did you see anything you like?"

"Huh?" Holly had no idea what he was talking about.

"Well," he said, "you've been staring at me all day."

"I have?"

"Looked like it to me. So I thought I'd invite you to do some more staring—up close and personal. Like down here by the lake tonight."

"Well, I, uh . . ." For a moment Holly didn't know what to say. As always when she was around Mick, she felt unsure of herself and a little frightened. But he was cute and she wanted to go. "Sure," she said. "Sounds like fun. I'll meet you after the campers are in bed."

That evening, while she waited on the dock, watching the moonlight sparkle on the lake, Holly thought about Mick. She really did like him, but there was something strange about him, something that didn't quite fit.

Maybe that night she'd find out what it was.

"Hi, Holly." Mick had come up so quietly she didn't see him until he sat down beside her.

"Mick!" she said. "You startled me."

"Looks like I'm always doing that," he said. He was wearing a tight white T-shirt over his cutoffs. He looked great—and he knew it.

"It's so beautiful out here," she said.

"Sounds like you're adjusting to camp," Mick said.

"I guess so," Holly agreed. "This is your second year as a counselor, isn't it?"

"Third," said Mick. "My second at Camp Nightwing."

"Why did you come back here?" she said.

He laughed. "Why not?" he said. "It's a great camp, even if Uncle Bill doesn't pay as much as some of the others. And it's close to where I live."

"Where's that?" said Holly.

"Believe it or not, a farm," said Mick with a little smile. "Not far from Belleville."

For a moment Holly was speechless. Mick seemed

so sophisticated that she had just assumed he was from a city. "I never knew that," she said.

"There's a lot you don't know about me," said Mick.

Holly just stared at him in the moonlight. He seemed so different then, not threatening or moody the way he usually was. Maybe she'd been all wrong about him. "I'd—I'd like to get to know you better," she said, meaning it in more than one way.

"That makes two of us," said Mick, his voice still gentle. Casually he laid his arm over Holly's shoulder.

"I mean," she said, inching away from him, "as a friend."

"No problem," said Mick, pulling her closer. "'Cause I feel really friendly right now."

This isn't working at all, Holly thought. She didn't want this—or did she? "Really, Mick," she said. "I do want to get to know you better, but more slowly." Firmly she pulled his arm away.

"Hey!" said Mick. "What is this? First you stare at me all day, then you say you want to get to know me better—"

"But I do!" said Holly. "Just not quite the way you have in mind."

"Well, that's just terrific!" said Mick. "You know something, Holly? I don't think you have any idea what you want!" He grabbed for her and pulled her close, bringing his face very near to hers.

Holly very much wanted Mick to kiss her, but she was frightened and knew that things were getting out of hand. "Let me go!" she cried, twisting away from him. With a lunge she pushed him away, and he fell off the dock and into the water.

He hit with a loud splash. Holly couldn't help laughing.

"I'm sorry!" she called to him. She held out her hand to help him up, but he shrugged it off.

"Forget it!" he said. "Next time you want to get to know me, I'll just send you a letter!"

He was so angry that Holly shrank back. She watched as he left the dock and ran up the path to the cabins.

Holly was walking back when a figure stepped onto the path in front of her. With shock Holly saw that it was Geri, her pale face twisted in a mask of fury.

"I saw and heard everything," Geri hissed. "I know what you're up to, Holly. I know everything!"

"I don't know what you're talking about!" cried Holly, involuntarily taking a step back.

"First you ruined my life back in Waynesbridge," Geri went on, her voice distorted with anger. "And now you're trying to steal Mick from me. Well, you won't get away with it, Holly. You won't get away with it!"

chapter
15

*T*he next morning, as she walked to the mess hall, Holly was in a daze. She had hardly been able to sleep after what had happened with Mick and Geri.

And she was still no closer than before to finding out what was going on in the camp.

"Holly, watch out!"

Holly raised her head just in time to see a softball coming straight at her.

"Oh!" she cried, dodging away.

"You kids be careful where you hit that!" Sandy called to some of the campers, then jogged over to Holly. "You okay?" he asked.

"Fine," said Holly. "Thanks."

"You seemed to be a million miles away."

"It's more like I *wish* I were a million miles away," said Holly.

"Still having trouble with the great outdoors?" he said sympathetically.

"It's more than that," said Holly. "It's . . . it's everything."

"Whoa," Sandy said. "Take it easy, Holly. Things can't be that bad. Want to talk about it?"

"Not really," Holly replied. "It's kind of personal."

"Oh," Sandy said, obviously hurt. "Sorry, I was just trying to help."

"I know that," Holly said. This place is a lunatic asylum, she thought. Why is everyone so touchy? She sighed. "I just—just didn't want to bore you with my problems."

"You won't bore me," said Sandy. "What's bothering you? Tell Uncle Sandy."

Suddenly Holly realized that she did want to talk about it. Part of what was wrong was that no one would listen to her. Uncle Bill was too busy, and Thea was too preoccupied with her problems with John.

"Why not?" she said. "Thanks." She followed him to a rock in the shade of a tree and told him about the three "accidents" and the red feathers. "I know it sounds crazy," she finished, "but I think someone is deliberately trying to destroy the camp." She thought about adding what had happened with the garter snake but decided that would make her sound paranoid.

"But why would anyone do that?" asked Sandy. "It doesn't make sense."

"I know," said Holly. "But maybe if I can find out who, I'll be able to figure out why."

"Maybe," said Sandy. But she could tell he didn't believe her. "Listen," he said after a moment. "I understand why you're worried. Anyone would be, and especially with Uncle Bill being your real uncle and all. Maybe the problem is just that you're too close to it."

"What do you mean?" said Holly.

"You spend every minute working with the campers and helping people. You're not even used to the outdoors yet. You haven't really had a chance to enjoy it. I think you'll see things differently when you're out of the camp."

"What are you talking about?" said Holly.

"The wilderness trip I'm leading next week," he said. "Didn't you know? You're assigned to the team as assistant boating counselor."

Wilderness trip? Now Holly remembered hearing some of the campers talking about it. But she'd been so busy she hadn't checked the duty roster to see who was going.

"It's just a few counselors and some of the advanced older campers," Sandy went on enthusiastically. "It'll be great."

"Wilderness?" said Holly. "Me?"

"You'll be a natural," said Sandy. "You're probably much better in the outdoors than you think you are."

"Well, I don't know," said Holly.

"It's just an overnighter," Sandy went on. "And Uncle Bill must think you can handle it, or he wouldn't have assigned you. Don't worry, Holly. It'll be fun. We get to canoe on the White River."

"Canoe? I thought all the canoes were dead," Holly said.

"No, we use rented ones we pick up at the campsite. It's easier than carting them all the way there. Really, you're going to love it. I promise."

Later, as Holly was on her way to the crafts cabin, she thought about the wilderness trip. Another thing to worry about! As she went past the main building, she could see Thea and John standing in the path. They seemed to be arguing. After a moment John stalked off, and Thea just stood still, stricken.

"Thea," Holly said, approaching her friend. "What is it?"

Thea looked as if she were fighting back tears. "It's John," she said miserably. "I finally asked him why he didn't meet me the other night. Do you know what he said?"

Holly shrugged.

"He said—get this—he said he had to write some letters! Did you ever hear of such a lame excuse?"

"Well," Holly said, "maybe he did. Or maybe he forgot and he was embarrassed to tell you."

"And maybe the moon is really made of green cheese!" said Thea. "No, I understand what's going on now. Namely, nothing. Obviously John doesn't care anything about me. Probably he never did! I feel like such an idiot!"

"I know how you feel," said Holly sympathetically. "That's one reason I decided to take a vacation from boys this summer."

"I feel like taking one for the rest of my life!"

"Come on, Thea," said Holly. "It's not like you were really going with John."

"Yeah, I know," said Thea. "And I guess I was half expecting something like this. But I feel like such a jerk."

"Well, don't, 'cause you're not. And there's plenty of other boys in camp."

"You should know," said Thea.

"What do you mean?" said Holly.

"Well," said Thea, with a trace of her old smile, "I heard you were down at the lake with Mick the other night."

"That was nothing," said Holly quickly, wondering if the whole camp was gossiping about her.

"And what about Sandy?" Thea went on.

"What about him?" said Holly, feeling increasingly uncomfortable.

"Every time I turn around, I see you talking to him. For someone on a vacation from boys you're really getting around."

"Sandy's just a friend," said Holly.

"Really?" said Thea. "I'm glad to hear it. Because I think he's really cute. And as soon as I get over my broken heart, I might check him out."

She gave an exaggerated wink and went off. Holly was glad to see that Thea was taking the "breakup" with John so well. She pushed open the door to the crafts cabin to find the girls sitting along a low wooden table, making simple, punch-type clay pots. In the center of the room Debra sat at the pottery wheel, putting the finishing touches on a vase.

"Sorry I'm late," said Holly, though she was only a minute or two late. Debra didn't answer but gave her a disgusted look.

Right, thought Holly. Well, she couldn't let Debra's negativity bother her, or she'd never get anything done. She took a deep breath and went to help the girls with their pots. They were all excited, especially Stacey, who wanted to paint a face on hers. Holly showed her how to do it, then began to explain to the girls how firing the pots in the kiln would make them hard.

"Like baking a cookie?" asked Jessica.

"A little like that," said Holly. "And it also brings out the colors of the glazes. This pot here," she said, pointing to an unfired pot, "doesn't look like much. But after it's fired in the kiln, it will be bright green, like this one." She held up a beautiful green pot with Debra's mark on the side.

"Ooh, let's see!" cried Stacey, jumping up and rushing to Holly's side.

"Careful," warned Holly. "It's very—"

But it was too late. Stacey had knocked it out of her hand, and the pot now lay in shattered pieces on the floor.

Debra jumped up from the wheel. "What have you done?" she screamed. "Can't you do anything right?"

For the rest of the afternoon Holly went about her duties almost mechanically, unable to turn her mind away from the terrible things she knew were happening. She felt more alone than she had in her life. No one would listen to her—not Uncle Bill, not even

Thea, who seemed to think Holly was just being paranoid.

Luckily, it was an unusually quiet afternoon. Most of the senior campers were in town at the local county fair. Half of the junior campers were on a picnic, so only Holly's group and three others were at the waterfront. After the last swim of the day Holly let the kids run on ahead, and she took the long way back to her cabin past the campfire circle.

She had reached the path that led to Cabin Five when a huge, ugly spider dropped down in front of her face. She jumped back, then saw Kit standing to the side of the path, dangling the rubber bug from a string.

Suddenly something inside of her snapped. "Why don't you grow up?" she shouted at Kit. "I've never done a single thing to you!"

"What about Geri?" he said with a nasty smile. "I hear you've done plenty to her."

"That's between me and Geri!" said Holly. "And besides—"

"I've got news for you," Kit cut in. "You're looking for real trouble. Not jokes."

Then his face changed, from sneering to menacing. Holly took a step back, and Kit stepped toward her.

"Leave me alone!" she cried as forcefully as she could. She ducked into the woods and began to run, finally stopping for breath in a small clearing.

And suddenly felt her arms being pinned from behind.

"Kit, you creep!" she said, struggling as hard as she could.

"Now, is that any way to talk?" said a different voice.

Mick's voice. It was Mick holding her.

"Let me go!" Holly cried, pulling against his strong arms. "What are you doing?"

"Inviting you to join our little party," said Mick, his voice calm and cold.

"She didn't like my invitation," said Kit, appearing in front of her, holding the fake spider.

"Too bad," said Mick. "Maybe she'll like the party favors better."

And now Geri stepped into the clearing. Her mouth was fixed in a mocking grin, and she was carrying a bucket in both hands.

Holding the bucket straight out in front of her, she began to walk slowly toward Holly.

"I know you're afraid of the outdoors, Holly," said Geri, still grinning nastily. "So here's your big chance to have all your nightmares come true."

Holly continued to struggle against Mick, but it was no use. How can this be happening? she wondered.

"Please," she said. "Please let me go."

"As soon as you've learned your lesson," said Mick. "As soon as you learn you're not better than everyone else."

Geri pushed the bucket right against Holly's chest. Inside it, squirming in shallow murky water, were half a dozen slimy leeches.

chapter
16

"**U**gh!" Holly cried in disgust and turned her head away.

"Like them?" said Geri. "We caught them just for you."

Next to Geri, Kit was laughing. And now Mick and Geri were laughing too, strangely excited laughs.

Holly told herself that they were only teasing her. But she couldn't forget that one of these three might be a very dangerous person. Or were all three dangerous—all three working together?

"You're always trying to make trouble, aren't you, Holly?" said Geri, as if reading her thoughts. "Well, we just want you to know that we don't appreciate your attitude!"

"Geri, I never did anything—"

"Don't say that!" Geri cut her off. "You deliberately tried to ruin my life two years ago. I told you then I'd get even. And now's my chance." She pressed the bucket harder against Holly.

"How does it feel, Holly?" Geri went on. "How does it feel to be helpless, to know that your life is in the hands of another person?" She was so close now that Holly could hear her breathing.

What's she going to do? Holly wondered.

For a very long moment Geri just stared at her, her face expressionless and cold. Then, abruptly, she turned away and crossed the clearing.

"Bring her over here, guys," Geri said.

Mick and Kit each grabbed one of Holly's arms and started pushing her toward a small creek that ran through that part of the woods.

"Miss Perfect. Miss Too Good for Everyone. You don't look perfect," said Geri. "You probably need a bath." And without warning she grabbed Holly's shirt and pushed her into the creek.

Holly fell hard, hitting her knee. There was very little water in the creek, so she plopped down onto the thick soft mud. It felt cold and clammy—and smelled of rotting leaves. I'm not going to let them see how scared I am, she told herself. No matter what else they do, I won't let them know I'm afraid of them.

She started to stand up to climb out of the creek, but lost her footing in the slimy mud and fell backward. Mick laughed harder. "It isn't funny when you're the one falling into the water, is it?"

"Will you cut it out!" Holly screamed. "This is so juvenile. I'd believe Kit would do something like this—but what's your excuse?" She stared at Mick coldly.

"Oh, lighten up," Kit said. "All the new counselors have to be initiated. It's a great camp tradition. Right, Geri?"

Geri ignored Kit's question. She stared at Holly with pure hatred.

"I think Holly's lonely," said Geri. "I think she needs some company in the water." She picked up the bucket of leeches and, before Holly could move, dumped it on her.

Holly screamed and tried desperately to scramble out, but the mud was too slippery and she kept falling.

"That's enough," Mick called to Geri, but he didn't make any attempt to help Holly up and out of the water.

Holly stared down. Two slimy leeches were squirming over her soaked T-shirt. She felt a sudden stinging in her leg and saw that another one had attached itself to her calf.

"No!" she cried. "No!"

This is a nightmare, Holly thought. It can't be happening.

Desperate, she turned to Geri, hoping to see some trace of the girl who had been her friend.

But Geri's face was cold, cold as the muddy water that was beginning to make Holly shiver.

And then she saw something over Geri's shoulder that made her even colder.

A fourth person was standing at the edge of the clearing, watching.

Sandy.

She couldn't be sure. The sun was in her eyes. But it *looked* like Sandy.

He was smiling too—a cruel, taunting smile.

"Help me!" she cried, feeling a leech crawl up her shoulder toward her neck.

When she raised her eyes again, Sandy was gone. Maybe she had just imagined him being there.

"How did you like the party, Holly?" said Geri. "Do you think you've learned your lesson? Do you promise to mind your own business from now on?"

They're going to let me go, Holly thought with relief.

"Or maybe we should teach you a *real* lesson," Geri went on.

Holly's heartbeat began to quicken again, finally pounding with her own terror.

"Come on, Geri, that's enough," said Mick suddenly. "It's late," he said. "We've got to get back. It's almost time for dinner."

Holly was surprised by his sudden reversal. He turned his head away, refusing to meet her eyes, then took Geri's arm. "Come on," he said.

With a last mean smile, Geri turned and walked off with Mick. Kit followed them like a puppy dog.

It's over, Holly thought.

She managed to climb out of the creek and then, her fingers quivering in revulsion, peeled the leech from her leg. It scarcely hurt at all, but a mottled red oval mark glistened on her bare skin. In sudden panic she felt her arms, and under her clothes, but no other leeches were clinging there.

Shakily she got to her feet and began to walk back to her cabin. She was cold and wet and miserable.

They didn't really hurt me, she thought. They only wanted to scare me.

Well, they succeeded.

But they'll never know. I'll never let them know how scared I was.

For just a moment Holly thought of telling her uncle Bill about what had happened. But, no, she decided. It would only make things worse, if he believed her at all.

Now she was more convinced than ever that one or all of the three—Mick, Kit, and Geri—knew something about what was going on in the camp. She wasn't being paranoid. They did want to hurt her, and it wasn't a joke! Just then her thoughts were cut off by a sudden terrified shriek.

"No! Please, no!"

chapter
_____
17

*H*olly stopped walking and stood in the dark woods, her heartbeat echoing in her ears.

The cry was not repeated, so she cautiously began to inch forward again.

Then, just as suddenly, the scream came again: "No!"

At that instant, Holly stepped into a small clearing and saw a flash of clothing as if someone were running away. A moment later she saw John as he appeared from behind a large oak tree.

"John!" she said, surprised. "What are you—"

"Holly!" he exclaimed, his voice sounding just as surprised. He swiftly moved his hand, and Holly thought he was hiding something behind his back.

"What's going on?" she said. "Who else is here?"

"Huh? Nobody," said John.

"I saw someone running," said Holly. "I just wondered—"

"No, really, I'm alone," said John, his voice becoming angry. "Why are you spying on me, anyway?"

"Spying?" Holly couldn't believe what she was hearing. "I'm sopping wet and covered with mud—the only thing I want to do is get back to my cabin."

"Yeah, yeah!" said John sarcastically. "Sure you were! Listen, I don't care if you *are* Uncle Bill's niece, if you don't leave me alone, you'll be sorry!"

"But I only—oh, forget it!" Frustrated, Holly stomped back toward her cabin. On top of everything else that had happened, now this.

What was going on with John, anyway? Why had he gotten so angry? Why was everyone angry at her?

It was getting late. She didn't want to get into trouble with Debra, so she started to run.

But before she could reach safety, she became aware of the sound of running footsteps. They were behind her and getting closer.

Was John coming after her?

She ran harder, and then, suddenly, someone collided with her. She felt strong arms reach around her from behind. She turned and stared up into the puzzled face of Sandy.

"Holly!" he said. "Sorry I almost mowed you down. What happened to you?"

"It's a long story, she said. "I—I was out walking and fell into a creek," she added, searching his face for any sign of guilt that he had helped Geri. She saw nothing.

"Are you all right?"

"Yes," Holly said wearily, seeing only friendship and concern on his face. She must have imagined she saw him by the creek.

"Are you sure you're okay?" Sandy repeated. "How did it happen, anyway?"

"I wasn't paying attention to where I was going, and I slipped," said Holly.

"That's all?" he said.

"Well, then afterward I ran into John," she admitted. "He sort of upset me. He acted like I'd caught him robbing a bank or something. He yelled at me and threatened me."

"Really?" said Sandy. He shook his head. "He's a very moody guy."

"I guess so," Holly said. "I can't even imagine what that was about."

"You're having a bad summer so far, aren't you?" said Sandy sympathetically.

"Not as bad as Uncle Bill," said Holly gloomily. "If only I could get him to listen to me. If only I could get *anyone* to listen to me."

"I know how you feel," said Sandy. "I mean, not exactly. But I know what it's like when you know something bad has happened and no one will listen to you."

"You do?" said Holly.

Sandy nodded. "Someday I'll tell you about it," he said. He smiled at her, and she began to feel relaxed and safe for the first time all day. For a moment they just gazed at each other, and then Sandy broke his eyes away to glance at his watch. "Hey," he said. "I almost forgot. I have something for you. I just got the final list of who's going on the wilderness trip." He reached in his pocket, then handed her a folded list.

"Thanks," she said. "See you at dinner."

The cabin was empty, and Holly let herself collapse on her bunk for a moment. As she began to undress for a quick shower, the list Sandy had given her fluttered to the floor. Idly she picked it up and scanned it.

The fifteen campers were all older kids she didn't really know.

But as she read the counselors' names, her heart began to pound again. In addition to Holly, Sandy, and Stewart Winchester, the archery instructor, the remaining counselors on the list were Mick, Kit, and Geri.

chapter
18

"*H*olly?"

It was Thea, gently rapping on the door. "Hey, are you in here?"

Holly was getting dressed for dinner. "How's it going?"

"Not wonderful," said Thea. "How about you?"

Briefly Holly told her friend about the latest trouble with Geri. "I just don't know what to do," she finished. "Geri is really out of control. She really scares me. And things with Debra are as bad as ever. This afternoon Jessica asked me why Debra and I don't like each other."

"That bad?" said Thea.

"It's getting so I try to think of ways to stay away

from her. Except that I'm her assistant, so it's nearly impossible."

"Maybe things will improve when she gets to know you better," said Thea sympathetically.

"Maybe," said Holly. "But I'm not holding my breath." She looked at her watch. "Hey, it's almost time for dinner. I wonder where Debra is? She always likes to be here to help the girls wash up."

"I don't know," said Thea. "I'm meeting my campers in the mess hall. I'll help you."

Holly went to the door and called her campers in. Then she and Thea helped them wash up. Jessica was sunburned and didn't want to wash her face, but Holly smoothed some cool ointment on it, and soon the little girl was smiling again.

If only, she thought, everything in camp could be as easy as working with the girls!

Walking to the mess hall, she searched for Debra. Where in the world could she be? She decided that Debra might be deliberately staying away to test Holly somehow.

If so, she thought, Debra is in for a surprise. Because so far I'm doing fine.

The mess hall was much noisier than usual, and Thea and Holly saw why as soon as they entered: hanging from one of the crossbeams on the ceiling was Kit, wearing a gorilla mask and dropping pieces of banana peel on the tables below.

Actually, it was pretty funny and, in spite of everything, Holly found herself laughing. "If he's trying to attract Geri's attention, she can't help but notice him," she said to Thea.

"You don't know Geri," said Thea. Both girls turned to where Geri was sitting, completely ignoring Kit, as if he were invisible. After a moment he threw a piece of peel at her, and it landed right in the middle of her tray.

"Kit, you dork!" Geri shouted, standing up. "That's not funny at all!"

"Ooga-ooga," said Kit and shinnied down a thick rope he'd tied to the crossbeam. Still wearing the mask, he approached Geri's table, but she was once again ignoring him.

"If he weren't such a jerk, I could feel sorry for him," said Thea.

"Debra isn't here," said Holly, suddenly aware that the senior counselor still hadn't shown up.

"Are you sure?" asked Thea. "That's not like her at all." She stood on her chair to search the hall, then shrugged. "You're right," she said. "And John isn't here, either, which is also a little weird."

"Do you think they're off together somewhere?" asked Holly.

"I hope not!" said Thea.

"But what—" Holly stopped a moment as a horrifying thought occurred to her. "Thea," she said, "what if—"

"What if what?"

"What if something else has happened? What if Debra and John are hurt?"

"Oh, Holly," said Thea. "Will you forget your wild theories? Probably they're both just finishing something up. Or they lost track of the time. Anyway, I promised myself I wasn't going to think about John anymore, and I'm not!"

"Well, I have to think about the camp whether I want to or not, and I'm going to make sure there's nothing wrong," said Holly.

"Okay," said Thea, still not acting worried. "If you run into John, give him a message for me. Tell him to drop dead."

Thea went to join her campers, and Holly stopped by the table for Cabin Five. She explained to the girls that she was going to find Debra so they could all eat together, then she hurried out of the building. Holly kept her eyes open for any sign of trouble.

But the camp appeared to be peaceful and quiet except for the soft chirp of tree toads and the faint rustling of leaves in the summer breeze.

She first stopped by her cabin, just in case Debra had returned. There was no sign of her or any sign that she'd been there.

Holly glanced toward the lake, but she couldn't see anyone.

Debra must still be in the crafts cabin, she decided finally. And then she remembered how absorbed Debra had been in working that day. She must have lost track of the time.

Holly couldn't suppress a little smile as she imagined telling Debra *she* was late.

When she reached the crafts cabin, she saw that it was dark, and she almost turned away. At the last instant she decided to check it out.

She swung the door open.

"Debra?" she called. "Debra, are you in here?"

The only answer was a strange, high-pitched humming noise.

Holly stepped all the way into the cabin, flipping on the light as she did.

And stopped in shock.

Everything in the room—the floor, the walls—was covered with bright red splatters.

Splatters of blood.

Blood that was flying from the spinning electric potter's wheel.

Holly continued to look, horrified and sickened. The wheel turned rapidly, on each pass rubbing away more of the thing slumped over it.

The thing that she saw had once been a human face, but was now a bloody mass of raw pulp.

chapter

19

*H*olly stood paralyzed in the doorway, unable to stop staring at the horrifying sight before her.

It was Debra who sat slumped over the table, her face nearly rubbed off by the potting wheel. Only the long black braids identified her as Debra.

"No," Holly moaned involuntarily. "No, please, no."

Her hands trembling, she unplugged the wheel, then approached Debra's body, hoping for any sign of life.

But Debra remained still, still as death.

Holly reached out to feel Debra's wrist for a pulse, but Debra's skin was already cool.

She wasn't going to wake up. Not ever.

Now that she was closer, Holly could see what had

happened. The little owl pendant that Debra always wore around her neck had gotten tangled in the wheel. It must have pulled her down. Must have strangled her.

Surrounding Debra was a jumble of craft supplies. Struggling against the wheel, Debra must have reached out frantically and pulled them down from the shelf right behind her. Everywhere she looked, Holly saw spilled paints, beads, feathers, leather thongs, and gimp.

She had died fighting, Holly thought. Fighting the wheel.

Or had Debra been fighting some*one,* someone who killed her?

The room began to spin and tilt. Holly felt dizzy. I'm going to be sick, she thought.

No, I'm not, she decided. She took a deep breath. Calmer, she began to think. When she had first found Debra, she had assumed that her death had been an accident. But now she wasn't sure.

How could Debra, who was so experienced, have had this kind of accident? It didn't make sense.

Not Debra. Not careful, professional Debra.

But who would want to hurt her? And why?

Maybe, Holly suddenly thought, this was connected to the other incidents. A chill traveled down her backbone.

It was more than an accident this time.

It was murder.

And it was *her* co-counselor who was dead.

A sudden sound behind her.

She jumped, uttering a shriek.

Turning, she saw that it was John Hardesty.

"Holly?" he said. "I saw the open door, and I wondered—" Instantly he stopped talking. His eyes widened and the color went out of his face.

"Oh, John!" Holly cried and ran to him. She fell into his arms, thinking for a moment she might faint.

"Wh-what happened?" John whispered.

"I don't know," said Holly. "I think Debra got her owl pendant caught in the pottery wheel. I was looking for her, and I found her, and . . . and . . ."

"Take it easy," said John, stroking her back. But his voice was shaking. "We have to get a doctor," he said.

"It's too late for a doctor," said Holly. And then another sickening thought occurred to her. "John— why weren't you at dinner?"

"What?" he asked, distracted. "Dinner? I had some things to do first. What difference does it make?"

"None, I guess," said Holly.

"Listen," John said, his voice still shaky. "Why don't you stay here with the—with Debra. I'll go get Uncle Bill."

"Sure," said Holly. She watched as John took off. Then, careful not to look at Debra again, she sat on a stool facing the door.

I don't believe this, she kept thinking.

Such a horrible death!

Maybe, Holly decided, she should have tried harder, done things differently, so she and Debra could have been friends. "I'm sorry, Debra," she said. Involuntarily she turned to the body again.

And froze.

She hadn't noticed before, but now that she was

sitting, she could see where the pendant had become pulled into the wheel.

And she could see that something was entwined with the pendant.

It was covered with blood—and worn down to just a stick by the wheel. But Holly was sure she knew what it was. What it had to be.

A red feather.

chapter
20

Dear Chief,

Guess what? I decided to take up pottery.

I found it worthwhile. Quite worthwhile.

I guess even the crafts counselor didn't know that making pots could be so dangerous. That pendant looked so nice around her neck—but not as nice as my two hands.

The local police came by for a while. They questioned everyone.

But they're sure it was an accident.

A tragic accident.

They didn't even notice my calling card.

And I left it right where they couldn't miss it.

Well, that's about all for now. What do you think, Chief? Should I kill the other one?

It's up to you.

Please write soon and let me know what you want me to do.

Yours forever,
Me

chapter
21

That night had been the longest of Holly's life. The police had come and questioned everyone until nearly three in the morning. And they were back early the next morning, scientific experts going over the crafts cabin one last time.

It was obvious that they thought the whole thing had been an accident. Everyone seemed to think so—except for Holly.

And Geri.

As Holly was on her way to breakfast, Geri suddenly grabbed her arm. Geri's face was splotchy from lack of sleep and crying. "Guess you're glad Debra's gone, aren't you?" Geri said nastily.

Holly was shocked. "Of course not!" she said. "I feel as bad as you do!"

"I'll just bet you do," said Geri. "I thought it was very interesting that *you* were the one who found Debra's body."

"She was my senior counselor," Holly said. "I was worried when she didn't show up at dinner."

"Come off it, Holly," said Geri. "Everyone in camp knows you hated her."

"I did not!" protested Holly, stung by Geri's accusations. "We didn't get along great, but I kind of liked her. And I never—"

"Never what?" said Geri, smiling nastily. "John says that when he walked into the crafts cabin, you were just standing there, staring down at her."

"I was in shock," said Holly. "I thought—" and then she stopped and abruptly turned away. "Forget it!" she said. She felt bad enough already.

She couldn't believe it. Now Geri was accusing *her* of being a murderer. She's probably blabbing it all over camp too, Holly thought.

Well, Geri was right about one thing. Debra's death wasn't an accident. And Holly knew it was up to her to convince the police.

She'd been waiting on the uncomfortable wooden chair outside Uncle Bill's office for nearly twenty minutes when a soft-but-no-nonsense voice called, "Come in."

Holly walked in to see a very tall man with pale skin and dark hair bent over a thick pile of papers on Uncle Bill's desk. "Holly Flynn?" he said, raising his head. "I'm Inspector Bradley. I understand you want to talk to me?"

Holly nodded. "I talked to Detective Reed last

night. But he was only interested in what I saw when I found Debra. I wanted to tell you about the other stuff that's been going on."

Bradley met Holly's gaze straight. "What stuff?"

Quickly, and trying not to sound nervous, Holly started to tell him about the red feathers she had found. But by the time she got to her theory about someone trying to destroy the camp, she could tell he wasn't really listening.

"Feathers, right," he said. "We'll take all that into account in our investigation."

"But it couldn't just be coincidence," Holly insisted. "There were feathers at all the so-called accidents. Please listen to me! I'm positive that—"

Bradley raised his hand, cutting her off. "I understand how upset you must be, Holly," he said. "Finding a dead body is one of the most shocking things that can happen to anyone. But we have investigated thoroughly, and for now we must conclude that Debra's death was an accident."

"What about the other things?" Holly said. "The cabinet, and the canoes—"

"That's all very suspicious, but I'm afraid as police officers we can't jump to conclusions. We need solid proof if we're to broaden our investigation. I appreciate your concern, and please feel free to call me if you see or hear anything else."

His words said one thing—but Holly knew he meant something else. He didn't believe her, and he had no intention of taking her seriously.

She found Uncle Bill working in the rec room and was about to try once again to convince *him*, but she could see by the exhausted look on his face that the last thing he'd want to listen to was her theories.

"Oh, Holly," he said when he glanced up and saw her. "You poor thing. I feel so bad that you had to find Debra that way. Are you okay? Listen, I've reassigned Geri Marcus to replace Debra in your cabin."

Holly just gaped at him. "You've what?!"

"Geri has a lot of experience. She's almost like a senior counselor, and the girls all like her," Uncle Bill went on, not noticing the shocked expression on Holly's face.

"But, Uncle Bill," she said, "Geri and I don't get along! Couldn't you move someone else?"

"Geri's the most qualified for the job," he said. "And I must say, Holly, you seem to be having trouble getting along with a lot of people. Don't we have enough real trouble without looking for imaginary problems?"

Holly's cheeks stung at her uncle's unfair accusation. "But Geri is the one who hates me!" she said. "It goes back to when we were living in Waynesbridge. We—"

"I don't care what it goes back to!" snapped Uncle Bill. "Can't you see I've got my hands full here? If you can't get along, fine, I'll send you home. It'll leave me shorthanded, but I can't make a special case for you. Is that what you want, Holly? To go home?"

"No," she said in a small voice. "I want to stay."

"Then act like it!" he said. "Please, Holly, don't you have better things to do than stand around here arguing?"

chapter

22

"So the next thing she knew, a huge, pale white hand dropped out of the attic and began chasing her around the house," Kit said.

"A what?" hooted Mick. "A *hand* chased somebody around?"

"Sure," said Kit. "It was disembodied."

"What did it do, crawl like a spider?" asked Thea sarcastically. "Or maybe it just flew through the air?"

"Will you let me finish the story?" said Kit, sounding hurt. He was wearing a pair of fake fangs and lisped slightly. Holly tuned out as he continued to drone on. She had never liked ghost stories, but Kit had convinced Uncle Bill to have a ghost story contest at that evening's cookout. Whoever told the scariest story was supposed to win a prize. It seemed like a crazy idea when there was so much *real* horror happening at the camp, but Holly hadn't protested.

It was a lucky break for her, she decided. If everyone was busy with the ghost story contest, no one would notice if she was gone for a while.

Holly had a plan. While everyone was occupied, she was going to sneak into the boys' area and search the cabins of Kit, Mick, and John. She didn't know what she was looking for, but she was desperate. If only she could find some clue—any information that might lead her to Debra's killer.

She sneaked another glance across the fire. John hadn't entered the ghost story contest. He sat away from the others completely absorbed in tying knots in a rope. The other counselors and campers were all attentively listening as Kit went on with his story.

Holly slowly edged away from the fire, trying not to draw attention to herself.

"Where are you going?"

Holly jumped, her heart missing a beat. It was Thea.

For a moment Holly considered telling her friend what she planned to do. But then she decided against it. After all, Thea didn't believe her suspicions either.

"I'm just going back to my cabin for a sweater," Holly lied quickly. "See you later."

She took off in the direction of Cabin Five, and then, when she was out of sight of the campfire, circled around to the other side of camp. Kit and John were assigned to Cabin Nine, which was off by itself at the edge of the woods. She'd start there.

The cabin was completely dark as she approached.

Behind her an owl hooted, and something made a crackling sound in the woods nearby. For a moment Holly considered giving up and returning to the campfire.

But she knew she had to force herself to go ahead. She felt that time was running out. Debra was dead—Debra her co-counselor.

The danger was getting close.

Would Holly be next?

She took a deep breath to steady her nerves, then clicked on her pocket flashlight. Slowly, making as little noise as possible, she swung open the cabin door.

It creaked eerily in the silence, and she stepped inside the darkened cabin. She swung the light around the room and saw that Cabin Nine was arranged the same way as Cabin Five.

The kids' bunks were on one side and the counselors' on the other.

She shone the light on the counselors' area, wondering which was Kit's. When she saw the ugly, grinning gorilla mask hanging over a bunk, she had her answer.

This is it, Holly, she told herself. She stepped over to Kit's bunk and slid open the top drawer of his cubby.

Somehow, she had expected Kit to be a total slob. But his drawer was completely neat, with all his shirts and underwear neatly folded and arranged. She lifted a couple of piles to see what might be underneath them but found nothing.

The next drawer revealed more carefully folded clothing. She opened the bottom drawer and there was more of the same, except for a huge green snake. This time it didn't scare her. She recognized it as the rubber snake Kit had scared her with their second day in camp.

The whole drawer was full of Kit's practical jokes. There were snakes, masks, rubber insects, a fake noose, and several items that she didn't recognize. Except for the snake, everything was in a bag or a box and neatly labeled.

She opened a couple of boxes at random, but they contained exactly what the labels promised: rubber spiders, a green wig, and itching powder.

Who would have guessed Kit would be a neat person? she asked herself. She poked around for a few more minutes, but there was nothing to find. Except for the gorilla mask over his bunk, the only personal thing was a box of stationery and some envelopes beneath a paperweight on the top of the cubby.

So much for Kit, she thought.

Now what about John?

Nervously she glanced at her watch. She'd been gone almost twenty minutes. Maybe Kit was still telling his stupid ghost story. In any case, nobody would be leaving the campfire for a little while longer. She hoped.

She moved over to John's bunk and began going through his cubby. Like Kit's, the first two drawers contained clothing, but it was all jumbled together in one big mess. She quickly pawed through the socks, underwear, and T-shirts, but saw nothing that didn't belong.

The bottom drawer was a tangle of miscellaneous items—some lengths of rope, swimming goggles, sev-

114

eral paperback books, and a small wooden box inlaid with tiny red and white tiles.

She took the box out and shone the flashlight on it, intrigued. She had never seen anything like it and wondered where he had gotten it. She tried to open the lid, but it wouldn't budge. And then she saw, on the front of the box, a tiny keyhole.

But where was the key?

Quickly she rummaged through the other drawers again but had no luck in finding the key.

Then she remembered something she had seen on a TV detective show, and ran her hand along the undersides of the drawers, in case something was taped there.

All she got for her trouble was a splinter.

Not expecting to find anything, Holly next scrutinized John's bunk and the slats under it.

She stopped when she felt a hard metal object taped to one of the slats.

Her hands trembling in excitement, Holly pulled the metal object free of the tape. It was a tiny key, just the size to fit the red and white box.

She sat down on John's bed and carefully fitted the key into the lock.

She froze as footsteps sounded outside the cabin.

Someone was coming.

Holly searched frantically for a place to hide when the door suddenly swung open, and there, illuminated in the pale moonlight, stood John.

chapter

23

John stretched slowly, then switched on the light. He was about to cross the room when he saw Holly and froze.

For a moment he just stared at her in shock. Then his expression changed to anger. "What are you doing?" he demanded at last.

"I—I lost something." Holly said the first words that came to her mind.

"You lost something in *here?*" John said in disbelief.

"I— Well, no. I thought Kit might have found it," said Holly. "I was just checking."

"Kit's bunk is over there." John pointed.

"Why aren't you at the campfire?" Holly blurted out.

"One of the campers got sick," said John. "I helped

take him back to his cabin. But why should I explain myself to you?"

"It's later than I thought," said Holly desperately. "I'd better be going now."

"Not so fast," said John, quickly stepping in front of her. "First tell me what you're doing in my cabin."

"I—I . . ." Holly trailed off. She realized how lame anything she said would sound, and especially since she was still holding John's small wooden box.

"Well?" said John. "You want to explain what you're up to? Did your uncle ask you to spy on me? Is that why you're always poking around? Are you a spy for Uncle Bill?"

"No, of course not," said Holly. She sighed. "I'm sorry," she said. "Uncle Bill has nothing to do with this. I was—searching your cabin."

"Why?" said John. "What are you trying to find?"

"I don't really know," said Holly. "Do you remember what happened the first day of camp in the rec room?" She quickly reminded John of all the disasters that had taken place—culminating in Debra's death. "And I'm sure that someone is doing all these things deliberately—to ruin the camp," she finished. "Only I don't know who. So I'm trying to find out."

John sat down on his bunk and looked at Holly as if she had just arrived from another planet. "Who do you think you are," he asked, "Nancy Drew? If you're so suspicious, why not just go to the police?"

"I tried to," said Holly. "When the detectives were here the other day. But they wouldn't listen to me. So I knew I had to find out what's happening by myself."

"And I'm your number-one suspect?" John said.

"Not really," Holly admitted. "I was more interested in Kit, but there was nothing suspicious in his bunk or dresser."

"Nothing like a locked box, you mean?" said John.

"Look, I'm sorry," said Holly, annoyed and a little ashamed. She handed John the box. "Please try to forget it, okay?"

John took the box, but as she stood to leave he blocked her way.

"Not so fast," he said.

"I *said* I'm sorry," Holly said.

John didn't move.

She hadn't realized how broad he was, and noticing the cold, flat expression in his eyes, she felt a little shiver of fear.

"Please," she said. "Please let me go now."

John continued to stare at her a moment, then his face changed. "I'll let you go—for now," he said. "But I want you to promise you'll never spy on me again."

"I promise," said Holly.

She turned again, but John clamped his hand on her arm—hard. "And one other thing," he said. "If you ever say anything about any of this—to anyone— you'll be sorry, Holly. Very, very sorry."

Walking back along the dark path, Holly felt more confused than ever. She had never really thought John might be the killer. But why was he so secretive about his locked box? And what had he been up to that afternoon?

And she still didn't know for sure about Kit. On the surface he seemed to be only a harmless practical joker. But she couldn't forget the nasty, gleeful look in his eyes when he'd tormented her that afternoon.

Who else could it be? Was it possible that it was someone who wasn't even in camp, someone who sneaked onto the property?

Nervously she looked over her shoulder. Nothing but trees and the shimmering reflection from the moon.

If it was someone from outside the camp, Holly realized, there'd be no way for her to find out. So she had to concentrate on the people in camp.

But who?

The path led right by Cabin Fourteen, which Mick shared with Stewart. The door was open, and cheery yellow light spilled out onto the path. Curious, Holly glanced in and saw Mick hunched over a table, writing.

She was about to go on when her eye caught something else, something red.

She stopped and stared.

There, hanging on the wall above Mick's table, was a set of colorful Native American rattles, held together with twisted yarn.

On the handle of each rattle was a band of decoration—made from red feathers!

chapter
24

Camp Nightwing

Dear Chief,

One of the counselors is getting suspicious. Too bad.

I can't have that. I can't have anyone interfering with the things I have to do.

Too bad she didn't mind her own business. But it's too late now.

She'll be next, Chief. But I'll wait for the canoe trip. I'll let you know how it goes.

Yours Forever,
Me

chapter
25

"What do you suppose this is about?" Thea was obviously very sleepy as she nibbled at a sweet roll.

Holly, sitting next to her in the mess hall, shrugged her shoulders. Nobody knew what was going on—just that Uncle Bill had awakened all the counselors early for a special meeting. The aroma of eggs and bacon was drifting out of the kitchen, and Holly realized how hungry she was.

The rest of the counselors were slumped sleepily around tables, quietly sipping coffee and eating doughnuts and pastries.

"I know what this meeting is about," Kit announced loudly. "It's to announce that I've been elected Most Popular Counselor."

"Right," said Mick. "And the next announcement is that they've discovered life on Jupiter."

"Get real," said Kit.

"Get a life," cracked Mick.

Holly tuned out the boys' voices. She had no idea why Uncle Bill had called the meeting, but she was sure that it didn't mean anything good.

As he walked into the mess hall, she felt even more nervous. It was obvious he hadn't slept all night. There were dark circles under his eyes, and his face was pale and drawn.

"Sorry to get you all up so early," Bill apologized to the counselors. Even his voice sounded tired, beaten. "I just wanted to take a few minutes to talk to you about the things that have been happening so far." He paused to take a sip of coffee, made a face, then continued. "Now, it's nobody's fault what's happened, but you might as well know that I'm just hanging on to this camp by a thread. After all the things that have happened, and especially after what happened to poor Debra, that thread has gotten thinner and thinner. So I just wanted to tell you . . ." He stopped again, and Holly could tell he didn't want to say what came next. "I just wanted you to know," he went on, "that if anything else goes wrong, I'll have to shut down the camp. So I really need your help. Please let's all work together as a team." Bill glanced in Holly's direction.

I wish it were that simple, Holly thought.

The counselors all listened in stunned silence. No one knew what to say. They'd never seen Uncle Bill so grim.

"That's all," Uncle Bill said hastily. "Now, you all enjoy your breakfast and have a good day with the campers." He turned abruptly and strode quickly from the room.

Holly followed him with her eyes, her heart almost breaking in sympathy. She knew how much the camp meant to him and how terrible he felt about Debra's death.

After Uncle Bill's announcement Holly didn't feel much like eating. She stopped in the breakfast line for two cups of coffee, then wandered over to her uncle's office. The door was open, and he was just sitting at his desk, staring into space.

"Uncle Bill?" He focused his eyes on Holly with a tired smile. "I brought you some fresh coffee," she said, setting the cups on his desk.

"Thanks, Princess," he said.

For a moment the two of them just sat in silence, sipping their coffee.

"I felt really bad about what you said just now," Holly said finally.

Uncle Bill shrugged. "I have to face facts," he said. "I've been waiting for a loan to come through to keep the camp going for the rest of the summer. But after what happened to Debra, I'm not sure about it. It definitely won't surface if anything else happens."

"But nothing that's happened is your fault!" Holly protested.

"That doesn't matter in business," Bill said. "All that matters is the bottom line, meaning how your business looks and how much money it's making."

"It's not fair," she said.

"Life doesn't have to be fair," said Bill. He turned to stare out the window a moment. "You know, Holly," he went on, "when I first saw this camp, I knew that it was the place for me. I knew that at last I could make a business work. How could I have been so wrong?"

"Maybe you weren't wrong," she said.

"What do you mean?"

"Maybe you would be making a success of it—if someone wasn't trying to stop you!"

He turned on her angrily. "Now, you're not going to start that stuff about a mysterious plot to destroy the camp, are you?"

"Just listen to me for a moment," she said. "That's all you have to do, just listen. I can prove—"

"I said forget it!" he said. "You've told me your theories before, and I told you what I think of them."

"All right," she said. "But—"

"No *buts,*" he said, still annoyed. "I think maybe it will be good for you to get away on the wilderness trip tomorrow."

"That's another thing I wanted to talk to you about," said Holly. "I'm not sure it's such a good idea for me to go—"

"What do you mean, it's not a good idea?" Uncle Bill bellowed, cutting off the rest of her sentence. "Are you questioning my judgment now?"

"Of course not!" Holly protested. "It's just that—" She stopped, not knowing what else to say. She couldn't tell Bill that she was afraid of the trip, afraid of Mick and Kit and Geri, afraid of what they might do.

"It's just that I don't get along so great with the other counselors who are going," she finished lamely.

"Well, maybe this will give you a chance to *learn* to get along with them," Uncle Bill said. "Now, I'm not going to argue about it. With Debra gone, you're the boating counselor now. So of course you should go."

"But what about the girls in Cabin Five?"

"They'll be involved all day tomorrow with junior field day," said Uncle Bill. "Marta is running that and Thea can stay in the cabin overnight. Believe me. I've got everything covered." He was no longer yelling, but his voice still betrayed his anger.

"Honestly, Holly," he said after a moment. "When I asked you to work here this summer, it was because I needed your help. Now, please—be a help. Go along with things for a change. Don't look for trouble."

I won't, thought Holly. But I'm afraid trouble is going to find me.

chapter
26

*T*he next morning Holly was up early, preparing for the canoe trip. She had scarcely slept the night before, unable to stop her mind from replaying all the things that had happened the last couple of days.

If only Uncle Bill would listen to her.

She hurried to the front parking lot, where Sandy was busy loading kids and equipment into the rickety camp bus. Luckily it was only about thirty miles to the White River. It didn't look as if the bus could make it much farther than that.

Sandy smiled at her. "Glad you're coming," he said. "I think you'll have a better time than you expect."

"I hope so," said Holly. "Anyway, it'll be different."

"More different than you think," said Sandy. "There's been a last-minute change. Stewart got sick last night, so John's replacing him."

"John!" said Holly, shocked.

"Yeah," said Sandy, sounding worried. "And I don't know how he got Uncle Bill to agree. He's not really into canoeing. He hates the water."

Maybe John's coming because he knows I'm going, Holly thought in horror. Because the wilderness trip might be the perfect place to get me alone and—

"Holly?" Sandy interrupted her thoughts. She realized he had been telling her something.

"Sorry," she said. "My mind's still asleep. What was it?"

"I'll put John in my canoe where I can help him. That leaves you and Mick together, okay?"

Mick? At the sound of his name a vibrant picture popped into her mind—those beautiful Native American rattles covered with red feathers!

Paddling down the White River, Holly wondered how she had managed to make so many enemies in such a short time. The other counselors were barely speaking to her.

When they had gotten on the bus, Geri had taken one look at Holly and exclaimed, "Oh, no! Can't I get away from you for a single minute?"

John had given her a cold look, then turned away, and even Kit had snubbed her. Mick pretended that he didn't even see her. Then he'd argued with Sandy about the canoe assignments. "Why can't I be with Geri?" he'd demanded.

"Because it'll work better this way," said Sandy, not at all upset, but not listening to any protests either.

As they paddled down the White River, Sandy's canoe was in the lead, with Holly and Mick bringing up the rear. The counselors went two to a canoe with the stronger canoer in the back. The campers' canoes held three. Holly watched Geri and Kit paddling together, the campers in the canoe next to them laughing and shrieking at Kit's antics as he pretended to drop his paddle or fall in the water.

"Will you cut that out!" Geri finally yelled, and Kit finally did settle down.

The kids really like Kit, Holly realized. She wondered why she had never noticed before.

She tried to strike up a conversation with Mick, but he was giving her the silent treatment, answering in monosyllables and grunts.

Once she turned around in the canoe, and she thought he was starting to say something, but then he shook his head and looked away.

At lunchtime Mick still hadn't said a word to her. He just helped the campers out of their canoes, then hurried to where Geri was setting out food for lunch. Thanks a lot, Mick, Holly thought sarcastically.

Most of the rest of the day was the same. Mick, Geri, and John ignored Holly as if she were invisible, and Kit continued to act stupid.

By late afternoon they had reached the campsite, and everyone was tired. Sandy took Kit and several of the campers to gather firewood while the others prepared the campsite.

Holly had nearly finished clearing out a shallow pit for the campfire when she picked up the faint sound of sobbing.

Had one of the campers been hurt?

She turned to the other counselors, but Geri and Mick were deep in conversation and there was no sign of John.

She directed Henry, the oldest boy camper, to keep working on the pit, then set off to find out what was wrong.

She followed the sound of crying away from the camp into the woods.

It was getting dark, and Holly suddenly realized that she didn't know those woods at all. Why hadn't she brought a flashlight?

The trees were dense, much denser than in the woods around Camp Nightwing.

Instead of the well-marked paths around the camp, there were only twisted, weed-choked trails.

What kind of animals live around here? she wondered.

Maybe she'd better go back to camp for her light.

But the sobbing suddenly became louder, sounded even more hopeless.

One of the campers is in trouble, Holly thought. I can't go back. I've got to help now.

Or could it be a trick? Was someone trying to lure her away from camp, into the woods, where—

"Hello, Holly."

Holly jumped at the sound of her name.

Silhouetted against a tree, his face pale in the fading light, stood John. In his hand, the dying light glinted off the shiny metal blade of a knife.

chapter
27

"John!" Holly cried, terror and surprise mingling in her voice.

"I might have known!" he said. "What are you doing here? I told you not to spy—"

"I'm not spying!" Holly shouted. Suddenly she was so angry she forgot the knife he was holding. "I heard someone crying, and I was coming to help!"

"The only way you can help is to turn around and go back to camp!" John said, raising the knife. "If you don't, I'll—"

"John, stop!" cried a girl's voice. A slim, pretty girl came around from the far side of the tree and put her hand on John's arm.

"Courtney!" It was Courtney Blair, one of the senior campers. "What—what are you doing here?"

"I'm warning you, Holly," said John. "This is none of your business!" He took a step forward.

"John, for heaven's sake, stop it!" Courtney took the knife out of his hand. "Don't pay any attention to John," she told Holly. "We heard you coming, and John thought it might be a bear or something." She folded the knife and handed it back to John. Sheepishly he put it in his pocket.

"But what are you doing here?" asked Holly. "It's practically dark. I heard someone crying and—"

"That was me," said Courtney. Now Holly could see the tears on her face. "John and I were having a—an argument."

"I'm sorry, Court," said John, putting his arm around her shoulder. "I didn't mean to make you cry."

Suddenly Holly understood. John and Courtney had been seeing each other, in defiance of camp rules. No wonder John was so secretive.

"I guess you've found us out," John said bitterly. "Courtney's fifteen," he went on. "I'm almost three years older. We met at my old high school, but Court's parents thought there was too much difference in our ages, and they wouldn't let us see each other."

"So you decided to meet here at camp?" Holly guessed.

"What else could we do?" said John. "We really love each other." He looked down at Courtney tenderly, then back at Holly. "When you ran into me the other day in the woods, we were arguing. I told Court that I couldn't stand all this sneaking around. I thought we should tell her parents the truth."

"I had no idea," said Holly. "I thought—I don't know what I thought."

"It's just not fair," Courtney spoke up. "I'm really close to my folks. I don't want to have to choose between them and Johnny. So I just kinda lost it. I was yelling no, over and over. Then I just couldn't take it anymore. I ran away."

"I heard you," Holly said simply.

"She dropped her bracelet," added John. "I was afraid you'd see it, so I hid it behind my back."

"So that's why you signed up for the trip at the last minute," said Holly. "To be with Courtney."

John nodded. "I had to see her again, find a way to make her understand," he said.

"What was in the box?" Holly asked, curious.

John blushed. "A picture of Courtney and some letters," he said. "I knew I didn't dare let anyone see them." He sighed. "It's really been rough. We know what will happen if anyone catches us, but we just can't stay apart.

"I know we can't really ask you this," said John. "But now that you know what's going on with me and Courtney, please, Holly, please don't tell anyone."

"I won't," said Holly. "But please cool it on this trip. I won't say anything. But I won't lie for you—I can't." Holly shuddered. Where had she heard those words before?

chapter

28

*H*olly awoke from a warm and cozy dream about shopping at the Division Street Mall back in Shadyside to find herself wet and cold and sleeping outdoors. She sat up and then saw Sandy kneeling over her, shaking her shoulder. "What—?"

"Shh!" he said, a finger to his lips. "You can sleep longer if you want," he whispered. "But I'm about to scout out today's river trip. I thought you might want to come with me and see the sunrise."

"Really?" said Holly. "You mean the sun's actually going to rise today?"

"Come on," Sandy urged. "It's not a good idea to go canoeing alone. We'll be back before the others wake up."

She stretched, a little stiff from sleeping on the

ground. She felt surprised and happy that Sandy trusted her in the canoe, and even better that he wanted to spend time with her. She realized that she liked him more and more all the time.

She quickly brushed her teeth and combed her hair, then joined Sandy at the side of the river where he was watching the sun rise over the mountains across the river.

"I love the early morning," he said. "I love the way the light bounces off the river and makes everything hazy."

Holly looked at the river, seeing it the way Sandy described it, and smiled. It was beautiful. He handed her a tin mug full of warm tea that they passed back and forth between them.

"What'll they think when they see we're gone?" she said.

"We'll be back before anyone wakes up," said Sandy. "What I want to do is scout downriver a little ways to where it forks." He pulled out a map and pointed at it while he continued. "One side becomes a rapids, and I want to see if it's safe for the campers."

"Rapids sound like fun," said Holly, surprised at herself and realizing at the same time that she meant it.

"See?" Sandy smiled. "I knew you were a wilderness camper at heart."

They finished their tea and stepped into the canoe, Sandy in the back where he could steer. They began paddling down the wide, fast-flowing river. "See over there?" Sandy pointed out a still, dark area at one edge of the river. "That's a great fishing pool. Whenever you have quiet pools like that in a river, that's where the big fish like to hang out."

Sandy knows so much about the wilderness, Holly thought. Uncle Bill was really lucky he got him as a counselor this year.

Early-summer wildflowers formed a colorful jumble along the banks of the river, and at a bend they saw a family of deer daintily drinking at the water's edge.

"This is so beautiful!" Holly said breathily. "I'm so glad I came on the trip!"

"I'm glad you like it," said Sandy.

The canoe continued to skim along the rushing water. Up ahead the broad channel narrowed.

"We're nearly at the fork now," said Sandy. "Get ready for a fast ride."

The current picked up abruptly, and Holly was suddenly splashed. "Wow!" she said. "This is fast."

"Not nearly as fast as it'll be when we get to the real rapids," said Sandy. "Just keep paddling."

Holly was beginning to wonder if she was experienced enough to keep up with him, but she soon fell into the rhythm of paddling and began enjoying it. The sights along the bank moved by faster and faster.

"We're getting awfully far from the campsite, aren't we?" she asked after a moment. "Won't it take a long time to get back to the others?"

"Don't worry about it," said Sandy. "I know what I'm doing. I know this river."

"You know the river?" said Holly, suddenly confused. "You mean from the map?"

"I mean I know it," he said. "See that clearing up

ahead on the right? I camped out there for two days last summer."

"But—I thought you told me you were in the desert last summer."

Sandy didn't answer for a moment, and when he did, his voice sounded strange. "I didn't mean *I* camped out here. My brother did. He told me everything about it."

"Oh," said Holly. And then she remembered something. "Wait a minute, didn't you tell me you're an only child?"

Again Sandy didn't answer right away. He began to paddle more slowly.

"Sandy?"

"Just forget what I said, all right?" he said. Holly realized that he was nervous and wondered what she had said to upset him.

"Sandy," she said gently. "I'm sorry. I didn't mean to pry into your private life. I was just curious, that's all."

"You're curious about everything, aren't you, Holly?" And again his voice sounded strange.

This is wonderful, Holly thought. The only person on the wilderness trip who doesn't hate me, and I'm making him mad. She couldn't think of anything else to say, and for a while they paddled in silence. The current of the river was getting faster and faster, and she thought she could hear the sound of the rapids ahead.

"Sandy?" she said. "I think I hear the rapids."

"Well, that's why we're here, isn't it?" he said. "To check them out."

He sounded angry. Again Holly was perplexed. "Please," she said at last. "Please tell me what's bothering you."

He sighed loudly, then spoke in that strange new voice. "I guess my problem is that I've been a little careless," he said.

"What do you mean?"

"But you've been careless too, Holly," he said, instead of answering her directly.

"What do you mean?"

He didn't answer, and suddenly, although she couldn't say why, she felt frightened. Frightened of Sandy.

"What do you mean?" she repeated.

"I mean," he said, "that you didn't tell anyone you were coming with me."

chapter
29

For a moment Holly thought she had misunderstood. "What are you talking about?" She turned around suddenly to look at him, the canoe tipping a bit to one side.

"I said you'd been careless," Sandy repeated slowly. "That you didn't tell anyone you were coming with me." He stopped paddling, and Holly could see tension in every line of his body.

What's going on? she wondered.

"I didn't tell anyone because you said we'd be back before they woke up," she said lightly. "Sandy, what's wrong?"

He didn't answer, and he didn't resume paddling. The canoe began to drift.

"Sandy, we're drifting," she said.

139

"Yes," he agreed. He resumed paddling, slowly. His voice sounded so strange, so remote. Was this really the same guy who had been so nice to her?

"Sandy, what's wrong?" she said. "Please tell me. You can trust me."

"I already told you," he said. "I was careless. And now you've been careless too. That's what happens at Camp Nightwing. People get careless."

"What are you talking about?" Holly still felt uneasy, but she was beginning to be exasperated. Was Sandy playing some kind of game with her?

"Carelessness," he said. "For instance, Debra. Debra was careless."

"Maybe she was," Holly said. "But I'm still not sure it was an accident. I don't see how she could have gotten her pendant caught in the wheel."

"That was this summer," said Sandy, his voice still strange. "I was talking about last summer."

"What do you mean?"

"Last summer Debra was careless on a canoe trip," Sandy said. "It was a wilderness trip just like this one. There were six counselors and fifteen campers, just like this one. Six counselors and fifteen campers left Camp Nightwing for the wilderness. Six counselors came back. But only fourteen campers. All because Debra was careless."

"Are you talking about—about the accident that happened last summer?" said Holly.

"It wasn't an accident," said Sandy. "An accident happens by chance. This one was caused—caused by Debra and her carelessness."

Holly felt the unease growing in her again. Sandy

wasn't making sense, and his voice was sounding stranger and stranger, almost robotlike.

"I never heard much about the accident," Holly said. "I just know that something happened to one of the campers."

"Don't say one of the campers!" said Sandy. "He wasn't just another camper. He was special. Really special. His name was Seth."

"So you were here last summer after all?" Holly said.

"No!" said Sandy. "Don't you listen to anything I say? I wasn't here. Seth was here. Seth, my brother."

Holly was completely confused now. She hadn't heard of anyone named Seth. And Sandy had told her he was an only child. This must be some kind of trick, she thought. But why?

"I wrote to my brother every day at camp last summer," Sandy said. "And I still write him every day. No matter how I feel, no matter how busy I am, I write him a letter." He paused, then went on, sounding sad. "But he hasn't answered in the longest time."

Seth is dead, Holly realized. Sandy's brother was the boy who died at Nightwing last summer.

"You would have liked him," Sandy continued. "He was just a great guy. Too bad you can never meet him."

"I never knew anyone named Seth," she said, just for something to say.

"He never liked the name," said Sandy, sounding harsh. "So I called him Chief. This was his sign." Sandy reached in his pocket. In his hand was a red feather.

chapter
30

*H*olly suddenly felt as if a cold hand had closed around her heart.

She was beginning to understand. To understand all too well.

"He was three years younger than me," Sandy went on. "But we were close. In fact, you could say he was my best friend. I was happy that he was going to camp here last year. But he never came home. He died here. Here in this river."

"That's awful," said Holly, sympathy mingling with her growing fright.

"All because Debra was careless," Sandy repeated. "But she has paid now. Paid for her carelessness."

Holly had never been so scared. Sandy killed

Debra. Sandy was a murderer and she was trapped in a little canoe with him.

"That's right," Sandy went on, as if reading her thoughts. "I was the one, the one who made Debra pay. I was the one who did the other things. Camp Nightwing is an evil place. It cannot be allowed to go on."

"I—I understand how you must feel," Holly said. She spoke as calmly as she could. She knew that a part of Sandy was kind, and rational, and as sane as she was. Maybe if she spoke calmly, she could reach that part and stop him from—whatever he was planning.

"You don't understand," Sandy said. "No one does."

"No, really," said Holly. "Really, I do. I mean, I love my sister, and I know how I'd feel if anything happened to her."

Sandy abruptly laughed, a cruel, mocking laugh. "But nothing *did* happen to her," he said. "Not like what happened to Chief. Do you know what I did when I found out? I made a vow. A sacred vow to Chief. I promised him that I would get even for what happened to him."

He had stopped paddling again, and the canoe was drifting, drifting in the swift current. Up ahead Holly could hear the rush of water that meant the rapids were coming up.

"I—I understand that too," said Holly. She hoped her voice didn't sound as scared as she felt. I've got to keep him talking, she thought. As long as he's talking, he won't do anything. "I mean, it's a natural reaction. But why make everyone pay for what only one person caused?"

"It was more than Debra!" Sandy answered immediately. "If there was no Camp Nightwing, Chief would still be alive. So everyone connected with the camp had to pay too. Don't you see?"

"Yes," said Holly. "Yes, I do. I do see, Sandy."

Sandy's face was distorted in an ugly look of suspicion. How could I have ever thought he was handsome? Holly wondered.

"You're just humoring me!" he shouted. "But it won't work. You know, I thought you were different, Holly. When you first came to camp, I liked you. I believed you were someone I could trust."

"You can trust me, Sandy," Holly said. "I only want to help you."

"It's no good," he said. He sighed, then went on. "At first I wasn't going to hurt you. Even when I found out you were Uncle Bill's niece, I still liked you. I tried to scare you away, by putting that snake under your pillow."

"You did that!" gasped Holly.

"I thought you'd get the hint and leave. I didn't want anything to happen to you," Sandy went on. "But you refused to leave. Instead you kept sneaking around, poking into things that weren't your business."

"I didn't know what was going on," Holly said desperately. "I was only trying to help Uncle Bill."

"Uncle Bill is just as much responsible for what happened to Chief as Debra was," Sandy said coldly.

"But I didn't have anything to do with it," protested Holly. "I wasn't even here last summer!"

"True," said Sandy. "But I can't let you go now. You know too much."

Holly's heart was beating so fast, she felt as if it might fly right out of her chest. She was alone on a rushing river with a crazy person, a murderer. She thought nothing could be more terrifying.

And then the canoe drifted around a bend—and the roaring rapids loomed ahead.

"Paddle!" Sandy commanded, almost sounding like himself.

Too terrified to protest, Holly turned around to the bow and started paddling. Sandy guided the boat into the right fork, directly into the center of the fast-running white water.

The noise of the rapids was so loud, Holly couldn't hear anything else. The cold, stinging water sprayed in her face and drenched her. For a moment she was so busy paddling she almost forgot where she was—and with whom.

She cried out as the canoe suddenly rammed into a rock. It spun all the way around before resuming its lurching progress through the white water.

Now it was rocking from side to side, tossed in the rushing water as if it were a piece of kindling. The canoe lurched hard to the left, and Holly thought for a moment she would be thrown out.

"Sandy!" she screamed. "Sandy!" She turned to face him. "Sandy! Get us out of this! We'll both be killed!"

Sandy didn't answer. Instead he started to laugh!

And then he tossed his paddle into the white water.

chapter
31

"What have you done?" Holly shrieked, but the words were lost in the deafening roar of the water.

Sandy kept laughing.

His paddle had already disappeared in the seething foam. Holly stared down into the water in terror. She tried to paddle, tried to straighten out the canoe, but the current was too strong.

Now Sandy was standing up, almost tipping the canoe over.

Her heart pounding furiously, Holly stared at him, hoping to see a spark of the old Sandy, a spark of sanity.

But all she saw was the mindless stare of the insane. He started to speak again and then began yelling. At first Holly couldn't understand what he was saying. But then by concentrating she could just make out the words.

"You're next, Holly!" he said. "You're next!"

And now she understood.

Understood that he meant to kill her—even if it meant killing them both.

"No!" she cried and shrank back as he began to advance to the front of the canoe, toward her.

"It's time for you to pay!" Sandy yelled. "Don't fight me. You don't have a chance, Holly."

"No!" she shrieked again. "No! Sandy, stop it! Let me go!"

He lunged toward her. Again the canoe tipped low into the water, and Holly had to grab the gunwales to keep from being thrown out.

Instinctively Holly grabbed up her paddle and swung it at Sandy. He ducked, then lunged for her again. She half stood, to get better balance, and swung again.

She felt the paddle connect with his head, with a sickening thud.

Sandy gazed at her open-mouthed, then fell into the bottom of the canoe.

Holly was so surprised, she didn't know what to do at first. She poked at Sandy with the paddle, but he didn't move.

Have I killed him?

For a moment she felt a little sick, but then she realized the most important thing was to get the canoe out of the rapids. Then she'd have to figure out how to get back to camp.

The rapids had picked up speed, and Holly was very careful as she sat back down. Just then the canoe hit a rock, then another.

"No!" she screamed.

She flew into the air and landed in the rushing water, choking and sputtering. Desperately she clawed at the metal of the canoe, but it swept away, leaving her fingernails torn and bleeding.

She fought to stay on the surface of the swirling, rushing water, then watched in despair as the canoe spun away down the river.

She looked around her frantically, but all she could see was white foam. The riverbanks looked impossibly far away.

She could feel the stirrings of panic begin to lick at the edge of her mind.

Calm down, Holly, she told herself. You're a good swimmer. Just stay calm and swim toward the shore.

Taking a deep breath, she struck out against the current. But between strokes, the current pulled her back to the middle of the river. No matter how hard she stroked, she didn't get any closer to the shore.

Keep calm, she told herself again and again. Swim diagonally across the current.

Gasping, struggling for each breath, she made slow progress. Soon she was out of the swiftest part of the current. She had only to swim across still water to the bank.

She rested a moment before looking upstream.

An enormous fallen tree was rushing straight for her on the foam of the river.

chapter
32

Holly screamed, taking in a large mouthful of water.

The fallen tree was only a couple of feet away.

She didn't have time to think, only react.

Filling her lungs with air, she dived, going as far under the water as she could.

Her lungs were on fire, her chest nearly bursting.

I've got to hold on, she told herself. I've got to.

Black spots began to dance before her eyes.

And she felt the tree's branches brush over her body, then, mercifully, move on down the river.

When she came to the surface she felt strangely calm, no longer frightened.

The only thing that was important now was her survival.

With all her strength Holly began to strike out for the shore, her arms moving strongly through the roiling water, her feet kicking in an even rhythm.

Every muscle in her body ached, but she kept moving, with a strength she hadn't known she possessed.

Just as she thought she couldn't swim another stroke, her feet brushed the rocky bottom, and she shakily walked to the bank.

Exhausted and shivering, Holly sat against a tree, catching her breath, trying to sort out her thoughts. Can all this really be happening? she wondered.

Sandy? Kind, considerate Sandy, who had shown her the beauty of the wilderness?

Holly realized that poor Sandy must have been driven insane by grief over his brother's death. She remembered the expression on his face when he talked about Seth, the almost gleeful way he had told her that Debra had paid for her "carelessness."

Where was Sandy now? Still in the canoe? He hadn't moved after she hit him, and the canoe was heading for the roughest of the rapids. She didn't know how long the rapids went on, and she imagined Sandy's body washed up on the shore miles downstream.

No! she told herself. Stop thinking that way! There was only one thing for her to do, and that was return to camp, as quickly as possible, and get help.

But how would she get back? It was a long way.

Through the woods. Alone.

She couldn't stay where she was. She was freezing cold from the icy water. Even as she thought about it, a shiver passed through her. I've got to keep moving, Holly told herself. It's still morning, and I'm strong. There's plenty of time to get back to the others. When she told them what happened, she thought, even Geri, Mick, and Kit would have to help her.

Holly thought briefly of trying to find a trail through the woods, but soon realized that was likely to get her lost. The best thing to do, no matter how difficult, would be to follow the riverbank, back the way she and Sandy had come.

She began walking, her shoes squishing along the muddy bank. The woods along the river were much thicker than those around Camp Nightwing, and she couldn't help thinking about some of the things she had heard about the Fear Street Woods behind her house in Shadyside. How the spirits of the dead sometimes roamed the woods.

Had she killed Sandy? Would his spirit roam the woods now? Would it come after her?

There was a sharp crackling noise just ahead of her, and Holly jumped in fright. Something big was moving toward the river.

And then she saw it: a doe, followed by her fawn, teetering on spindly legs.

Holly sighed in relief and watched the two deer as they made their way down to the water. Somewhere a mockingbird began to trill, and suddenly the woods were just woods again, full of animals and birds rather than spirits of the Undead.

Feeling a little better, Holly began to walk faster. The path along the river became narrower as low hills began to rise. It was very beautiful, all green and peaceful, the loudest noise the rushing river.

Holly fell into a gentle rhythm of walking, not even thinking much now.

There was another crackling noise, behind her this time, and Holly hoped she would get to see another deer.

But the crackling changed to thumping, and she realized it was footsteps. Running footsteps.

In terror Holly froze, turning toward the direction of the sound.

The trees parted and a human stepped out in front of her.

It was Sandy.

chapter

33

*H*olly stepped back and screamed.

Sandy remained still, a faint smile on his face. "What's the matter, Holly?" he finally said. "You look as if you've seen a ghost."

"But you were—you were in the canoe!" she gasped. "I thought you were—"

"Dead?" said Sandy. "Is that what you thought? And that I'm a ghost, coming back to haunt you?"

For a moment that was exactly what Holly had thought.

"I'm alive, all right," Sandy said. He rubbed his hand over his head where Holly had hit him with the paddle. "But it's no thanks to you. You tried to kill me, Holly."

"No!" she cried. "No, I didn't! I didn't mean to hurt you!" She took another step backward.

"Do you know what?" he said. "I believe you. You're a good, kind person, Holly. But I won't let you stop me from what I have to do."

"How—how did you get back here?" she asked, trying to keep her voice from shaking.

"I'm a good canoer," Sandy said. "A super camper, like my brother, Chief. I must have been unconscious for only a few moments. I took your paddle and brought the canoe over to the edge of the river. Then I started paddling back, to find out what had happened to you."

Holly couldn't think of anything else to say. She took another step backward. Sandy took a step toward her.

"I watched you," he said. "I saw you struggling in the river. I thought maybe you would drown, and then I wouldn't have to worry about you anymore."

"You don't need to worry!" she said. "I won't say anything to anyone, I promise."

"You're just saying that," he said. "Because you're scared."

"No!" she protested. "I mean it!"

He shook his head, the faint smile still on his lips. "It's too late, Holly," he said. "We've both gone too far. When I get through with you, I'll go back to camp and tell everyone that there was another boating accident. Another tragic accident, like the one that happened last year."

"No," Holly murmured. "No, please."

"They'll all believe me," Sandy went on. "And when they find out, that will be the end of Camp Nightwing. Just the way I promised Chief."

"No, no, no," Holly kept saying, even though she knew it would do no good.

Sandy took another step toward her, swooped down, and picked up a thick tree limb.

Holly watched in horror as he raised it and began to swing it at her. She finally moved and broke into a run.

Behind her she could hear Sandy, close behind, breathing hard.

Her only hope was to duck into the woods, to hide from him. Ignoring the rocks and raised tree roots that tore at her bare legs, she began to run through the woods. Low branches stung her face, but she couldn't stop to look for a clear path. She could do nothing but run.

Run, and try to ignore the pounding footsteps behind her.

She slipped once and managed to scramble to her feet just ahead of Sandy. She thought she heard him laughing as he came after her.

Her breath was coming in gasps now, and she knew she couldn't go much farther. And then, suddenly, just ahead she saw a steep unwooded hill. If she could climb it, get to the other side . . .

But the rocks on the hill were slippery with early-morning dew, and she was only partway up when she saw Sandy was right beneath her.

He swung the branch with all his force.

Holly felt it connect with her left foot.

A shock of pain.

And then the foot went numb all the way to her toes.

She scrambled a bit farther up and saw Sandy picking up the branch again, preparing to climb after her.

Desperate, Holly raised her eyes. Just above her, a small cave was cut into the hill. If she could manage to wriggle into it, she might be able to fend Sandy off and protect herself.

Summoning her last ounce of strength, Holly lunged upward and wriggled into the mouth of the cave.

And stopped.

Ahead of her, coiled in a writhing mass just inside the cave entrance, was a nest of hissing snakes.

chapter
34

*S*eeing her, the snakes began to uncoil. Holly froze for a moment, panicked.

Behind her, she could hear Sandy scrabbling up the slope.

Even if the snakes hadn't been there, she realized now, the cave was much too small to hold her. Her panic turned to despair, to the desire to just give up and let whatever would happen, happen.

No! she told herself. No! The unclouded part of her mind pushed the panic away, told her she had a chance, one chance.

But could she do it? The snakes slithered closer, and Holly felt her body begin to tremble uncontrollably.

Sandy had reached the cave now, and she suddenly

felt his hand grip her ankle, causing a searing pain to shoot through her whole leg.

Do it, Holly! she told herself.

Holly reached out, grabbed the nearest snake, then turned and heaved it in Sandy's face.

Startled, Sandy let out a cry.

He lost his footing.

And fell backward down the hill, his arms and legs flailing wildly as he tried to break the fall.

At last he stopped rolling and lay at the bottom of the hill, unmoving.

Trembling all over, Holly wriggled out of the cave and stared down at Sandy. Was it a trick?

No.

His face was deathly pale, and one of his arms was twisted unnaturally beneath him.

She began limping down the hill, down to where Sandy lay. When she got to the bottom, she could see that he was breathing. A trickle of blood ran down his forehead.

For a long time Holly just stood still, knowing she had to get back to the camp, to get help. She was trembling and felt cold all over.

You can do it, Holly, she told herself. It's not that far. You can make it back in plenty of time.

She took a deep breath, then started walking back to the river.

And stopped in horror as the trees parted again.

There, standing directly in front of her, was Mick.

"No!" she screamed aloud. "No, no, no!" She couldn't stand it. After everything, after escaping from Sandy, now Mick was after her.

159

"Holly! Holly! What is it?"

She became aware that Mick was calling her name, and now she faced him. He wore a look of shock.

He wasn't trying to kill her. He obviously didn't know what had happened.

"Oh, Mick!" she cried. And suddenly crumpled into his arms.

The faint wail of a siren faded into the distance as the ambulance took Sandy away, away from the campsite, away from all the horrors of the past week.

Holly, wrapped in a blanket, shivered as she watched the flashing red light retreat down the long graveled road. Mick, sitting beside her, handed her a cup of hot broth, and she gratefully took a sip. She had told Mick the whole story of what Sandy had done, then helped as well as she could while he dragged Sandy's unconscious body back to the river and loaded it into the canoe. She had been so exhausted she had barely been able to paddle, but Mick had managed to return them to the campsite, where the bus would come to pick them up.

She pulled the blanket tighter around herself. She couldn't stop shivering. She had never been so cold in her life.

"Are you okay?" Mick asked with concern.

Holly nodded. She took another sip of the warming, strengthening broth. "There's one thing I don't understand," she said at last, her voice no longer shaking. "How did you happen to find us?"

Embarrassment crossed Mick's face, and he looked at the ground before answering.

"I couldn't sleep last night," he said. "I—I had a lot of thinking to do. I felt really bad about what happened the other day. And about the way we've all been treating you. I tried all day to find the words, but I just couldn't. I wanted to tell you I'm really sorry. I mean, I was kind of mad at you for what happened earlier. But that's no excuse. This may sound weird, but I really do like you a lot."

Holly felt sympathetic to Mick. She could see how hard it was for him to admit that he'd been wrong.

"But why did you follow me and Sandy?" she asked, puzzled.

"Well, as I said, I decided I wanted to apologize to you. I thought I'd talk to you early in the morning before the others woke up. But then I saw Sandy come and talk to you, and when the two of you went off in the canoe, I decided to follow, just to see what you were up to."

"So you were right behind us all along?"

"No," said Mick. "I'm not nearly as good a canoer as Sandy, especially alone, so I got farther and farther behind. I was about to head back when I saw your canoe tied up by the shore. I was curious, so I tied mine up next to it, and then the next thing I knew I ran into you in the woods."

"I'm glad you did," Holly said. "Thanks, Mick."

When the camp bus arrived, Uncle Bill ran to Holly and took her in his arms. He seemed to have aged ten years in the past day.

"How are you feeling, Princess?" he asked Holly.

161

"I'm all right now," she said. "What will happen to Sandy?"

"He'll get the help he needs," Uncle Bill said sadly. "I just didn't know. Can you imagine he actually killed Debra? Strangled her. I had no idea. Seth—the boy who died last year—was his stepbrother. They had different last names. How could I have known they were related?"

"It wasn't your fault," Holly said. "None of it was."

"The police found a stack of letters in Sandy's room," Uncle Bill went on. "They were all addressed to Chief. Turns out that was Seth's private nickname."

"What about feathers?" Holly said. "Did they find any red feathers in Sandy's things?"

"Oh, yeah," Uncle Bill said. "There was a whole stash of them, in a box under his bunk. You were right about that after all."

"So it's all over," Holly said quietly, gratefully.

"Yes. Maybe now Camp Nightwing can go back to being a happy place again," her uncle said.

Holly hugged him and started back to her cabin to change. "Hey, wait up," someone called. She turned on the path to see Mick hurrying after her.

"How are you doing?" he asked, his face filled with concern. "You okay?"

"Yeah, I am." She smiled at him. "Thanks to you."

"Aw, shucks," he said with exaggerated modesty. He started to say something else, but a bright green snake dropped out of a tree onto the path at their feet.

"Hey!" He leaped backward to avoid stepping on it. Holly bent down, nonchalantly picked up the snake, and tossed it into the woods. "It's just a snake," she said, smiling at him playfully.

"Wow," Mick said, his mouth open in surprise. "I'm impressed. You've changed, Holly. I think you're catching on to this place."

"Yes, I think I am," Holly agreed. "And I think from now on I'm going to like it here."

"Me too," Mick said quietly. He put his arm around her, and they wandered happily up the path to their cabins.

About the Author

R. L. STINE is the author of more than twenty mysteries and thrillers for Young Adult readers. He also writes funny novels and joke books.

In addition to his publishing work, he is Head Writer of the children's TV show "Eureeka's Castle."

He lives in New York City with his wife, Jane, and son, Matt.

WATCH OUT FOR

THE SECRET BEDROOM
(Coming in September 1991)

Lea Carson is new to Shadyside, new to school, and new to Fear Street; and although she doesn't want to believe it at first, she may soon be Fear Street's newest victim. There is someone or something trapped in the boarded-up attic above Lea's bedroom. What evil lies behind the attic door? Will Lea be strong enough to resist? The answer will be revealed when the secret bedroom is finally opened.